"There's One More Thing That We Haven't Covered."

"What would that be?" For the life of her, Summer couldn't imagine what there was left to be decided after their many conversations on the subject.

"We're going to start acting like we're a couple," Ryder stated.

"You mean, as if we've fallen in love?" Things just kept getting more complicated with every conversation they had.

"It's easier to go with that than it is to try and explain everything." He leaned over and briefly pressed his lips to hers. "Besides, that's what people are going to think anyway. We might as well go along with it."

"Does that mean we'll be openly affectionate toward each other?" she asked, liking the way his kiss made her feel warm all over.

"Yup. That's what people do when they're… involved."

She frowned. "Do you think we can be convincing?"

"Let's see..." he said.

Dear Reader,

Best friends are those special people in our lives that we share almost everything with. They are there for us when we need them to listen and keep our secrets, help out when two sets of hands are better than one and even though they know our worst faults, they love us anyway. Most times, close friends are the same gender. But I've always been intrigued by the idea of a man and woman sharing this special bond.

The second installment of The Good, The Bad and The Texan series, *A Baby Between Friends* explores what happens when a woman asks her best friend for the ultimate favor. Will Ryder McClain and Summer Patterson be able to remain friends when she asks him to help her have a baby or will their relationship evolve into something much deeper?

So please sit back and enjoy the ride as we find out what happens when daytime friends become nighttime lovers and the cool autumn nights become hotter than a west Texas Fourth of July.

All the best,

Kathie DeNosky

KATHIE DENOSKY

A BABY BETWEEN FRIENDS

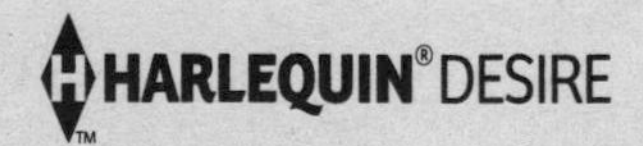

ISBN-13: 978-0-373-73255-5

A BABY BETWEEN FRIENDS

This edition published by arrangement with Harlequin Books S.A.

For questions and comments about the quality of this book, please contact us at CustomerService@Harlequin.com.

Printed in U.S.A.

Books by Kathie DeNosky

Harlequin Desire

In Bed with the Opposition #2126
Sex, Lies and the Southern Belle #2132
**His Marriage to Remember* #2161
**A Baby Between Friends* #2242

Silhouette Desire

Cassie's Cowboy Daddy #1439
Cowboy Boss #1457
A Lawman in Her Stocking #1475
In Bed with the Enemy #1521
Lonetree Ranchers: Brant #1528
Lonetree Ranchers: Morgan #1540
Lonetree Ranchers: Colt #1551
Remembering One Wild Night #1559
Baby at His Convenience #1595
A Rare Sensation #1633
†*Engagement Between Enemies* #1700
†*Reunion of Revenge* #1707
†*Betrothed for the Baby* #1712
The Expectant Executive #1759
Mistress of Fortune #1789
†*Bossman Billionaire* #1957
†*One Night, Two Babies* #1966
†*The Billionaire's Unexpected Heir* #1972
Expecting the Rancher's Heir #2036

Silhouette Books

Home for the Holidays
"New Year's Baby"

†The Illegitimate Heirs
*The Good, the Bad
and the Texan

Other titles by this author
available in ebook format.

KATHIE DENOSKY

lives in her native southern Illinois on the land her family settled in 1839. She writes highly sensual stories with a generous amount of humor; her books have appeared on the *USA TODAY* bestseller list and received numerous awards, including two National Readers' Choice Awards. Kathie enjoys going to rodeos, traveling to research settings for her books and listening to country music. Readers may contact her by emailing kathie@kathiedenosky.com. They can also visit her website, www.kathiedenosky.com, or find her on Facebook, www.facebook.com/Kathie-DeNosky-Author/278166445536145.

This book is dedicated to my editor Stacy Boyd
for allowing me to spread my wings and soar.

One

Ryder McClain's temper flared as he stared at the five men grinning at him like a bunch of damned fools. Having spent their teen years together on the Last Chance Ranch, a home for boys that the foster care system had labeled lost causes, he loved all of them. In all ways except by blood, they were his brothers. However, at this moment, nothing would be more satisfying than to wrap his hands around their throats and throttle every one of them.

"I'm only going to say this one more time and then I expect you all to drop it," he said through gritted teeth. "I brought Summer Patterson to the party tonight because she's a friend who didn't have any other plans. Period. There's absolutely nothing going on between us."

"Sure, if you say so, bro." Jaron Lambert's skeptical expression indicated that he didn't believe a word Ryder had just said. "And I'll bet you still believe in the Easter Bunny and the Tooth Fairy, don't ya?"

"I'll give you all a hundred-to-one odds that the lady in question has other ideas," Lane Donaldson said, rocking back on the heels of his handcrafted Caiman leather boots. A highly successful, professional poker player, Lane used his master's degree in psychology to read people like an open book. In this instance, the man was definitely reading the wrong chapter.

"Yup. I'd say she's cut you from the herd and getting ready to measure you for a saddle," Sam Rafferty added, laughing. The only married one of his foster brothers, Sam and his wife, Bria, were throwing the party to celebrate the renewal of their wedding vows, as well as Bria's pregnancy. "You might as well face it, Ryder. Your bachelor days are numbered."

"You're just hoping one of us will join you in the pool of the blissfully hitched," Ryder said, blowing out a frustrated breath. "But as far as Summer and I are concerned, that's not going to happen—now or in the future. Neither one of us have any intention of being anything more than best friends. End of discussion."

Smiling, T.J. Malloy paused with his beer bottle halfway to his mouth. "Ryder, did you get kicked in the head by a bull at the last rodeo you worked? That might explain you not being able to see what's as plain as your hand in front of your face."

"Well, now, this makes things a whole lot easier for me," Nate Rafferty said, smirking as he turned toward the dance floor where Summer stood talking to Bria and her sister, Mariah. "As long as you're not interested, I think I'll just mosey on over there and ask the little lady to dance."

Ryder knew that his brother was baiting him, but without a second thought, his hand came down like a vise-grip on Nate's shoulder. "Don't even think about it, Romeo."

"Oh, so you *have* staked your claim," Lane said smugly.

"No, I haven't." Ryder's jaw was clenched so hard that he wouldn't be surprised if it took a crowbar to pry his teeth apart. "But Summer doesn't need Nate's brand of grief." He thought the world of his foster brother, but Nate Rafferty had a love 'em and leave 'em philosophy that had left a string of broken hearts across the entire Southwest and then some. "No offense, Nate, but you're the last thing she needs."

"He's got you there, Nate," Sam said, nodding. The only two biological siblings of the group, Sam and Nate couldn't have been more different. The older of the two, Sam had never even come close to having the wild streak that his younger brother Nate had.

Nate shrugged. "I can't help it if I love the ladies."

"You take your interest in women to a whole other level," Ryder said, shaking his head in disgust. "Leave this lady alone and we'll get along just fine. Cross that line and you and I are going to have one hell of a big problem, bro."

He chose to ignore the knowing looks his brothers exchanged and, in favor of doing them all bodily harm, walked away. For one thing, he didn't want to ruin Sam and Bria's reception by getting into a knock-down, drag-out brawl. And for another, he made sure he never raised a fist in anger to anyone for any reason. He had been down that road once, when he was a teenager, and the results had damned near ruined his life. He wasn't going to risk going down it again.

"Ryder?"

Turning at the sound of the familiar female voice, he watched the pretty blond-haired woman with the bluest eyes he had ever seen walk toward him. He and Summer had been best friends for the past few years, and although any man would be lucky to call her his woman, Ryder had avoided thinking of her as anything but his friend. Anything more between them and he would feel obligated to tell her the reason he had finished growing up at the Last Chance Ranch. That was something he didn't care to share with anyone and why he didn't intend to enter into a serious relationship with any woman. Some things were just better left buried in the past. Besides, he didn't want to take the chance of losing the easygoing friendship they had forged by becoming romantically involved with her. He suspected she felt the same way.

"Is something wrong?" she asked, her expression reflecting her concern.

Letting go of his anger, Ryder shook his head as he smiled at the petite woman standing next to him. "No, I just got tired of listening to my brothers' bull."

She smiled wistfully. "You're lucky. At least you have brothers to irritate you. I've never had that problem."

Ryder felt as guilty as hell. As aggravating as his foster brothers could be at times, there wasn't a doubt in his mind they would all be there for him no matter what—the same as he would be for all of them. They meant the world to him and there wasn't a day that went by he didn't thank the good Lord above that he had them in his life.

But Summer had never had anything like that. Over the course of their friendship, he had learned she was the only child of an older couple who, during her senior year in college, had been killed in the small plane her father owned. With their deaths, she had been left with no family at all.

"Yeah, they sure can be a thorn in my side sometimes." As the last traces of his anger dissipated, he grinned. "But I guess after all these years I don't have any other choice but to keep them."

She laughed. "Good idea, cowboy. But seriously, your family is great. I know some of your brothers from seeing them compete at the rodeos we've worked, but I'd never met Sam's wife and her sister. They're very nice and I think it's wonderful that you all have stayed so close over the years."

When Ryder noticed Nate eyeing Summer like a fox sizing up an unguarded henhouse, he shot his brother a warning glare, then asked, "Have you had a chance to dance yet?"

"Only the line dances," she answered, glancing at the dance floor Sam had his hired hands construct in one of the barns for the celebration.

"I thought I saw Sam's head wrangler ask you to dance a little earlier," he said, frowning.

"I suppose he was nice enough," she replied, shrugging one slender shoulder. "But I wasn't in the mood to dance then."

"Well, if you don't mind a cowboy with two left feet and the worst sense of rhythm this side of the Mississippi, I'd be honored to stand in one spot with you and sway in time to the music," he offered.

Her eyes filled with humor. "I thought all Texas cowboys took pride in sashaying around the dance floor doing the two-step or the stroll."

"You know me better than that, darlin'." As the band started playing a slow, dreamy country tune, he shook his head in mock disgust and placing his hand to her back, guided her out onto the dance floor. "This is one Texan who doesn't sashay, prance or shimmy anywhere. Anytime. Ever."

"I beg to differ with you," she murmured, placing her hands on his biceps when he rested his at her trim waist. "I've seen you when you're dancing with a two-thousand-pound bull. You have some pretty smooth moves, cowboy."

"That's because it's my job." He shrugged and tried to ignore the warmth of her soft palms burning his skin through the fabric of his chambray shirt. "If I don't get those old bulls to dance with me, a bull rider gets run over."

"Don't you have a degree in ranch management?" she asked. "I would have thought you'd be content to stay home and run your ranch instead of traveling around the country playing chicken with a bulldozer on hooves."

"Yup, I'm a proud graduate of Texas A&M." He put himself between her and a couple enthusiastically two-stepping their way around the dance floor in an effort to keep them from bumping into her. "But I have a good, reliable foreman I pay quite well to check in with me several times a day. He gives me a full report on how things are going, I tell him what I want done and he sees that it's taken care of. That frees me up to be out on the rodeo circuit saving knuckleheaded bull riders like Nate and Jaron."

As Summer gazed up at him, she frowned. "I don't think I've ever asked, but why did you choose to be a rodeo bullfighter instead of a rider?"

"One time when our foster dad, Hank, was teaching us all to rodeo, one of the training bulls got loose and tried to mow down Jaron. I didn't have a clue what I was doing, but I jumped in the arena and put myself between the two of them to keep that from happening. It turned out that I was pretty good at distracting a bull and getting it to chase me." He shrugged. "I've been doing it ever since."

"In other words, you like being a hero," she said, smiling.

Laughing, he shook his head. "Nah. I'm in it for the adrenaline rush, darlin'." It was an easier explanation than admitting that he had always felt compelled to protect others from danger at the risk of his own safety.

When the song ended, Ryder led her off the dance floor and after finding an empty table for them, made sure she was comfortably seated before he went to get them a couple of drinks. He frowned as he made his way to the bar. His arms still tingled where she had rested her hands, and for the life of him, he couldn't figure out why. That had never happened before. Had his brothers' ribbing put ideas in his head about Summer?

As he continued to ponder the strange sensation, he looked up to see his brothers watching with no small amount of interest. They all wore the same sappy, know-it-all grin, making him want to plant his fist in all of their guts.

Ryder was extremely grateful that their foster father had instilled a strong sense of family among the boys he helped guide through their troubled teenage years. As Hank Calvert always told them, once they were grown they would appreciate having each other and a little bit of history together that they could look back on since none of them had any other family to speak of. And that's the way Ryder felt…most of the time. But at other times—like right now—having brothers could be a real pain in the ass.

As Summer waited for Ryder to return with their drinks, she absently watched the dancers form a couple of parallel lines and begin to move in unison to a lively tune. She couldn't get over how much she was enjoying herself. Normally she turned down all invitations from the men she worked with, no matter what the occasion or the circumstances. But Ryder was different. They had been best friends from the time she took the job as public relations director for the rodeo association southwestern circuit, and for reasons she couldn't explain, she trusted him. He was honest, didn't play the games that most men did, and despite his above average height and muscular build, she didn't feel at all threatened by him.

Of course, that might have something to do with the way he had run interference with some of their more aggressive male coworkers when she first started working for the rodeo association. From the day they met, Ryder had made it a point to remind all of them that she was a lady and should be treated as such. He had shown her nothing but his utmost respect, and it hadn't taken long before they had developed an easy, comfortable relationship. And not once in all the time she had known him had he indicated that he wanted anything more from her than to be her friend.

Unfortunately, she couldn't say the same for a lot of the men she knew. Most of them fell into two categories—blatant flirts who made it clear what they wanted from a woman, and the seemingly harmless type who lured a woman into a false sense of security before revealing their true hidden agenda. It was the latter group that was the most dangerous. The flirts were easy to spot and, once rebuffed, usually moved on to set their sights on another female. But the men with hidden agendas were nothing more than predators hiding behind a facade of sincerity.

As she absently stared at the dancers, a shiver slithered up her spine. Regrettably, she had learned that lesson the hard way. But it was one she never, as long as she lived, intended to forget.

"Would you mind if I join you, Summer?" Bria Rafferty asked, from behind her. "After that last dance, I need a minute or two to catch my breath."

Turning to glance over her shoulder, Summer smiled at the pretty auburn-haired woman. "Please have a seat." She looked around. "Where's the rest of the clan?"

"Sam, Nate, T.J. and Lane are in a lively debate about the differences between breeds of bucking bulls and which ones are the hardest to ride." Bria laughed as she pointed to the other side of the barn. "And Mariah and Jaron are arguing again about whether I'm going to have a boy or a girl."

"What are you and Sam hoping to have?" Summer asked, smiling when Bria lowered herself into the chair across from her.

"I don't care as long as the baby is healthy," Bria said, placing her hand protectively over her still-flat stomach.

"What about your husband?" Summer was pretty sure she already knew the answer. "What does Sam want?"

The woman's smile confirmed her suspicions. "Sam says he doesn't care, but I think he's secretly hoping for a boy."

Summer smiled. "Isn't that what most men want?"

"I think it's because men want a son to do things with, as well as carry on their family name," Bria answered.

"Not to mention the fact that females of all ages are a complete mystery to most men and they'd rather not have to deal with raising a child they can't understand," Summer added.

Grinning, Bria nodded. "Well, there is that."

While one of her guests stopped to congratulate Bria on her pregnancy, Summer couldn't help but feel envious. Nothing would please her more than to have a child of her own—a son or daughter to love and to love her in return. She had been so lonely since her parents died that she craved that sense of belonging again, that connection with a family. Having a child of her own would help restore some of those ties and if the plan she had come up with over the past six months worked, she would accomplish just that.

"When is your baby due?" she asked as the guest moved on.

"In early spring." Bria glowed with happiness and Summer knew it had to be because she had just entered her second trimester. Ryder had mentioned that almost a year ago Bria and Sam had lost a baby in the early weeks of pregnancy—a baby they had both desperately wanted.

"It won't be too much longer and you'll know for sure whether you're having a girl or a boy." She hoped one day in the very near future to experience the joys of expecting a child herself and learning if she would be having a son or daughter.

"Sam and I have decided we don't want the doctor to tell us." Bria laughed. "But the closer it gets to having the sonogram, the more I think Sam is going to change his mind."

"Why do you say that?"

"He keeps asking me if I feel like I'm carrying a boy." The woman rolled her eyes. "Like I would know."

"Men just don't have a clue." Summer marveled at the misconceptions some men had. "If there's a bigger mystery to a man than a woman it has to be pregnancy."

Grinning, Bria nodded. "Exactly."

"Would you like for me to get you something to drink, Bria?" Ryder asked, returning to the table. He handed a soft drink to Summer, then set a bottle of beer on the table in front of the empty chair beside her.

"Thank you, Ryder. But I think I'm going to go see if Sam is ready to cut that humongous cake he insisted we had to have." Bria rose to her feet. "I'm pretty sure he wanted to support the old saying that everything is bigger in Texas."

Summer glanced over at the giant, four-tiered cake in the center of the refreshment table. "The cake is beautiful, but I have to agree with you. It's definitely worthy of the axiom."

"I hope you have plenty of room in the freezer," Ryder added, chuckling as he pulled out the chair and sat down. "From the size of it, I'd say you're going to have about half of it left over."

Nodding, Bria flashed a smile. "I won't have to make a birthday cake for any of you for at least another year. I can just thaw out some of this one, put a candle on it and sing 'Happy Birthday.'"

"She makes each of us a dinner and a cake for our birthday," Ryder explained as Bria walked across the barn toward her husband. "All of us that is except for Jaron. He's crazy for her apple pie, so she makes a couple of those for him and sticks a candle in the middle of them."

"I think it's wonderful that you're all so close," Summer said wistfully.

Having spent the past several years alone on her

birthday and holidays, she coveted Ryder's family gatherings. She was sure if he had known, he would have insisted that she join them. But she hadn't let on because she didn't want that, hadn't wanted to be reminded of all that she had lost. That was the main reason she had taken the job of the on-site PR person for the rodeo association. She was constantly on the move from one town to the next coordinating the many rodeos held throughout the southwestern circuit, and she was always so busy that she didn't have time to think of how lonely her life had become. She was, however, glad that Ryder had invited her to his family's celebration tonight. It made her more certain than ever that she had made the right decision to start her own family.

"Did your foster father celebrate with you all before he passed away?" she asked, curious to hear about how they had come together and bonded as a family.

"Bria made sure to include Hank and her sister, Mariah, in all of our get-togethers," Ryder replied. "Family is everything to Bria and we all appreciate that. It helps us stay close and in touch with what's going on with each other."

Watching Ryder from the corner of her eye, she admired him and his foster brothers for the change they had made in their lives and the tight-knit bond they had formed. They might have been brought together because of their troubled youth, but with the help of a very special man, they had all learned to let go of the past and move forward. Through dedication and hard work, all six of them had become upstanding, highly successful men, and in the process, they had remained just as close, if not closer, than any biological siblings.

When Bria and Sam finished cutting the beautiful Western-themed cake, then invited their guests to have some, Ryder rose from the chair beside her. “I’ll go get us a piece of cake, then if you’d like we can dance a few more times before I take you back to the hotel.”

“That sounds like a pretty good plan, cowboy,” she said agreeably.

He had invited her to spend the weekend at his ranch, but she had decided against it, opting to stay in a hotel room in a nearby town instead. For one thing, speculation about their friendship had already surfaced with some of the other rodeo association contract personnel on the circuit, and she didn’t feel the need to supply the busybodies with more fodder for their rumor mill. And for another, she wanted to discuss her future plans with Ryder on the drive back from the party. Depending on his reaction, staying at the Blue Canyon Ranch with him could become a bit awkward.

An hour later, after congratulating the Raffertys once again on their renewed nuptials and Bria’s pregnancy, Summer let Ryder help her into the passenger side of his pickup truck, then anxiously waited for him to come around and climb into the driver’s seat. This was the part of the evening she had anticipated for the past two weeks—ever since making the decision to ask for his help.

“Are you cold?” he asked, sliding into the driver’s seat. “I can turn on the heater.”

“No, I’m fine. But thank you for asking.” There was

a little nip in the evening air, signaling that autumn had arrived, but she had been too distracted to notice.

"I hope you had a good time," he said, starting the truck and steering it down the long drive toward the main road.

"I really enjoyed myself," she reassured him with a smile. "Thank you for asking me to attend the party with you."

When Ryder turned onto the highway, he set the cruise control then turned on a popular country radio station. "You'll have to come back for one of our birthday get-togethers sometime."

"I'd like that," she said, realizing she meant it.

They fell into a comfortable silence and while Ryder drove the big dual-wheeled pickup truck through the star-studded Texas night, Summer studied his shadowed profile. If she'd had any doubts about her choice before attending the party with him, watching him throughout the evening had completely eradicated them. Ryder McClain was the real deal—honest, intelligent, easygoing and loyal to a fault. And it was only recently that she'd allowed herself to notice how incredibly good-looking he was.

With dark brown hair, forest-green eyes and a nice, effortless smile, he would be considered extremely handsome by any standards. But combined with his impressive physical presence and laid-back personality, Ryder McClain was the type of man most women fantasized about. His wide shoulders and broad chest would be the perfect place for a woman to lay her head when the world dealt her more than she felt she could handle. And the latent strength in his muscular arms as he held her to him would keep her safe and secure from all harm.

"Summer, are you all right?" he asked, startling her.

Slightly embarrassed and more than a little disconcerted with her train of thought, she nodded. "I was just thinking about the evening and what a nice time I had," she lied, unsure of how to start the conversation that would either help her dream come true—or send her in search of someone else to assist her.

"I can't think of any of our get-togethers when we haven't had a lot of fun," Ryder said, beaming.

"Even when your brothers irritate you like they did tonight?" she teased.

His rich laughter made her feel warm all over. "Yeah, even when we're giving each other a wagonload of grief, we still enjoy being together."

"From what you said earlier, I take it you were the one in the hot seat this evening?"

She was pretty sure she knew the reason they had been teasing him. Due to the demands of both of their jobs there had been very few occasions she and Ryder had been seen together anywhere but at one of the many rodeos they both worked. It was only natural that his brothers would speculate about their relationship, the same as their coworkers had done when she and Ryder started hanging out regularly at the rodeos they were working.

He shrugged. "As long as they're bugging me, they're leaving each other alone." Grinning, he added, "A few months back, we were all on Sam's case about what a stubborn, prideful fool he can be."

"Was that when he and Bria were having a rough patch in their marriage?"

"Yup."

"Do you always know that much about each other?" If he agreed to help her, she wasn't certain she would be overly comfortable with his family knowing about it.

"It's hard to hide things from the people who know you better than you sometimes know yourself," he acknowledged.

"So you don't keep any secrets from each other? Ever?"

"There are some things that we don't tell each other, but not very many." Turning his head to look at her, he furrowed his brow. "Why do you ask?"

She had purposely waited until they were alone in his truck and it was dark so she wouldn't have to meet his gaze. But the time had come to make her case and ask for his assistance. Considering the state of her nerves and the gravity of her request, she only hoped that she would be able to convey how important it was to her and how much she wanted him to help her.

"I've been doing a lot of thinking lately..." she began, wishing she had rehearsed what she was about to say a bit more. "Although I've never had a sibling, I miss being part of a family."

"I know, darlin'." He reached across the console to reassuringly cover her hand with his much larger one. "But one day, I'm sure you'll find someone and settle down, then you'll not only be part of his family, you can start one of your own."

"That's not going to happen," she said, shaking her head. "I have absolutely no interest in getting married, or having a man in my life other than as a friend." Ryder looked taken aback by the finality in her tone. They had never discussed what they thought their futures might hold and she was sure her adamant statement surprised him. Making sure her words were less vehement, she added, "I'm going to choose another route to become part of the family I want. These days, it's quite common for a woman to choose single motherhood."

"Well, there are a lot of kids of all ages who need a good home," he concurred, his tone filled with understanding. "A single woman adopting a little kid nowadays doesn't have the kind of obstacles they used to have."

"I'm not talking about adopting a child," Summer said, staring out the windshield at the dark Texas landscape. "At least not yet. I'd really like to experience all aspects of motherhood if I can, and that includes being pregnant."

"The last I heard, being pregnant is kind of difficult without the benefit of a man being involved," he said with a wry smile.

"To a certain degree, a man would need to be involved." They were quickly approaching the moment of truth. "But there are other ways besides having sex to become pregnant."

"Oh, so you're going to visit a sperm bank?" He didn't sound judgmental and she took that as a positive sign.

"No." She shook her head. "I'd rather know my baby's father than to have him be a number on a vial and a list of physical characteristics."

Ryder looked confused. "Then how do you figure on making this happen if you're unwilling to wait until you meet someone and you don't want to visit a sperm bank?"

Her pulse sped up. "I have a donor in mind."

"Well, I guess if the guy's agreeable that would work," he said thoughtfully. "Anybody I know?"

"Yes." She paused for a moment to shore up her courage. Then, before she lost her nerve, she blurted, "I want you to be the father of my baby, Ryder."

Two

Never at a loss for words, Ryder could only remember a couple of times in all of his thirty-three years that he had been struck completely speechless. At the moment, he couldn't have managed to string two words together if his life depended on it. Summer asking him to help her have a baby was the last thing he'd expected.

To keep from driving off into a ditch, he steered the truck to the side of the road, shifted it into Park, then turned to gape at the woman seated in the truck beside him. How in the world was he supposed to respond to a request like that? And why the hell was his lower body suddenly indicating that it was up for the challenge?

Shocked, as well as bewildered, his first inclination had been to laugh and ask her who it was she was really considering. But as he searched her pretty face, Ryder's heart began to thump against his ribs like a bass drum in a high school marching band. He could tell from the worry lines creasing her forehead that she wasn't joking. She was dead serious and waiting for him to tell her he would father her child.

"I know this comes as a bit of a surprise," she said, nervously twisting her hands into a knot in her lap. "But—"

"No, Summer," he said, finally finding his voice. "An unexpected gift or winning a few bucks in the lottery is a surprise. This is a shock that rivals standing in ankle-deep water and grabbing hold of a wire with a few thousand volts of electricity running through it."

She slowly nodded. "I'm sure it was the last thing you expected."

"You got that right, darlin'."

Ryder took a deep breath as he tried to figure out how to proceed. He knew he should ask some questions, but he wasn't entirely sure what he wanted to know first. What made her think that she wouldn't one day meet the right guy to change her mind about getting married and having the family she wanted? Why had she decided that he was the man she wanted to help her? And how did she figure she was going to get him to go along with such a cockamamy scheme?

"We're going to have to talk about this," he said, deciding that he needed time to think. Starting the truck's engine, he steered it back onto the road. "We'll stop by the hotel long enough for you to get your things and check out of your room. Then we'll drive on down to the Blue Canyon."

"No, I think it would be better if I stay at the hotel

instead of your ranch," she said, her tone adamant. "It might look like we were—"

"Seriously?" He released a frustrated breath as he glanced over at her. "You're worried about what people might think, but yet you want me to make you pregnant?"

"That isn't what I'm asking," she said, shaking her head. "I don't want you to *make* me pregnant. I'm asking you to put a donation in a cup for a clinical procedure in a doctor's office."

Ryder grunted. "Don't you think that's splitting hairs? The bottom line is, you'd be pregnant and I'd be the daddy."

"Oh, I wouldn't expect you to support the baby or help raise him or her," she insisted. "My parents left me more than enough money so that I never have to worry about taking care of myself and a child."

He barely resisted the urge to say a word she was sure to find highly offensive. Did she know him at all? She wanted him to help her make a baby and then just walk away like it was nothing?

Not in this lifetime. Or any other for that matter.

"Summer, we're going to wait to finish this conversation until after we get to my ranch," he said firmly. He needed time for the shock of her request—and the irritation that she didn't want him to have anything to do with his kid—to wear off before he was able to think rationally.

"No, I'd rather—"

"My housekeeper, Betty Lou, will be there with us so you don't have to worry about how things are going to look," he stated, wondering why she was so concerned about gossip. It wasn't like there wouldn't be plenty of that going around if he lost what little sense he had and agreed to help her—which he had no intention of doing. But he needed to get to the bottom of what she was thinking and why she was willing to risk their friendship to make her request.

He cleared his throat. "You'll have to admit that what you're asking of me is pretty massive, and we need to talk it over—a lot. Staying at my ranch until we have to take off for the next rodeo in a couple of days will give us the privacy to do that."

She didn't look at all happy about it, but she apparently realized that going to the Blue Canyon Ranch with him was her best chance of getting what she wanted. "If that's the only way you'll consider helping me—"

"It is."

He didn't want to give her any encouragement or mislead her into thinking he was going to assist her. But he needed to talk to her and make her see that there were other alternatives to have the family she wanted besides going around asking unsuspecting men to help her become pregnant.

She took a deep breath then slowly nodded. "All right. If you won't consider helping me any other way, I'll go to your ranch with you."

They both fell silent for the rest of the drive to the hotel and by the time she gathered her things, checked out and they drove on to the Blue Canyon, it was well past midnight.

"It's late and I don't know about you, but I'm pretty

tired," he said when he turned the truck onto the lane leading up to his ranch house. "Why don't we get a good night's sleep, then we can hash this all out after breakfast tomorrow morning?"

She nodded. "I suppose that would probably be best."

Parking in the circular drive in front of the house, Ryder got out and walked around to open the passenger door for her. "I guess before we go inside I'd better warn you. You'll need to steer clear of Lucifer."

"Who's that?" she asked, looking a little apprehensive.

"Betty Lou's cat," he answered, reaching into the back of the club cab for her luggage while she gazed up at his sprawling two-story ranch house.

"Oh, I won't mind being around him," she said, turning to smile at him. "I adore animals."

Ryder shook his head. "You won't like this one. I'm convinced he's the devil incarnate."

"Why do you say that?"

"He barely tolerates people." Ryder carried her bag to the front door, then letting them into the foyer, turned to reset the security system. "He hisses and spits at everyone who crosses his path, except Betty Lou. And there are times I think she walks on eggshells around him."

"You get chased by the biggest, meanest bulls the stock contractors can offer on a regular basis…and you're afraid of a house cat?" she asked with a cheeky grin.

Relieved that the awkwardness that followed her request seemed to have been put aside for the moment, he shrugged as he led her over to the winding staircase. "I know what to expect with a ton of pissed-off beef. But that cat is a whole different breed of misery. He's attitude with a screech and sharp claws. Sometimes he likes to lurk in high places and then, making a sound that will raise the hair on the head of a bald man, he drops down on top of you as you walk by." Ryder rotated his shoulders as he thought about the last time Lucifer had launched himself at him through the balusters from the top of the stairs. "He's sunk his claws into me enough times that I'm leery of walking past anything that's taller than I am without looking up first."

"Then why do you allow your housekeeper to keep him?" she asked when they reached the top of the stairs.

He'd asked himself that same question about a hundred times over the past several years—usually right after the cat had pounced on him. "Betty Lou thinks the sun rises and sets in that gray devil. She adopted him from an animal shelter after her husband died and when she took the job as my housekeeper, I didn't think it would be a big deal for her to bring him along with her. I like animals and besides, I'm gone a lot of the time anyway, so I don't have to be around him a lot."

"That's very nice of you," she said, sounding sincere. "But it's your house. You shouldn't have to worry about being mauled by a cat."

Ryder shrugged. "I don't see any reason to be a jerk about it when Lucifer means that much to her. I just try to steer clear of him as much as possible when I do make it home for a few days." Stopping at one of the guest bedrooms, he opened the door, turned on the light for her, then set her luggage beside the dresser. "Will this be all right? If not, there are five other bedrooms you can choose from."

He watched her look around the spacious room a moment before she turned to face him. "This is very nice, Ryder. Did you decorate it?"

Her teasing smile indicated that she was awaiting a reaction to her pointed question. He didn't disappoint her.

"Yeah, right. I just look like the kind of guy who knows all about stuff like pillows and curtains." Shaking his head, he added, "No, I hired a lady from Waco after I bought the ranch to come down here and redecorate the house."

"She did a wonderful job." Summer touched the patchwork quilt covering the bed. "This is very warm and welcoming."

"Thanks." He wasn't sure why it mattered so much, but it pleased him that she liked his home. "I bought it right after I sold my interest in a start-up company my college roommate launched while we were still in school."

"It must have been quite successful," she said as she continued to look around.

He grinned. "Ever heard of The Virtual Ledger computer programs?"

"Of course. They have a program for just about every kind of record-keeping anyone could want." Her eyes widened. "You helped found that?"

He laughed out loud. "Not hardly. I know just enough about a computer to screw it up and make it completely useless. But my roommate had the idea and I had some money saved back from working rodeos during the summers. I gave it to him and he gave me 50 percent of the company. Once it really took off, I sold him my interest in the company and we both got what we wanted out of the deal." He took a breath. "He has total control of The Virtual Ledger and I have this ranch and enough money to do whatever I want, whenever I want, for the rest of my life."

"Then why do you put yourself in danger fighting rodeo bulls?" she asked, frowning.

"Everybody has to have something that gives them a sense of purpose and makes them feel useful. Besides, I have to watch out for boneheads like Nate and Jaron." When she yawned, he turned to leave. "Get a good night's sleep and if you need anything, my room is at the far end of the hall."

Her smile caused a warm feeling to spread throughout his chest. "Thank you, Ryder, but I'll be fine."

Nodding, he quickly stepped out into the hall and closed the door behind him. What the hell was wrong with him? Summer had smiled at him hundreds of times over the past few years and he had never given it so much as a second thought. So why now did it feel like his temperature had spiked several degrees?

He shook his head as he strode toward the master suite. Hell, he still hadn't figured out why his arms had tingled where she rested her hands when they danced at the party. And why did the thought of her wanting him to be her baby daddy make him feel twitchy in places that had absolutely no business twitching?

* * *

When Summer opened her eyes to the shaft of sunlight peeking through the pale yellow curtains, she looked around the beautifully decorated room and for a brief moment wondered where she was. She was used to awakening in a generic hotel room where shades of beige and tan reigned supreme and the headboard of the bed was bolted to the wall. But instead of spending the night in a hotel as she'd planned, she had agreed to accompany Ryder to his ranch.

Her breath caught as she remembered why he had insisted she come home with him. After weeks of trying to find a way to bring up the subject and ask him to be the donor for her pregnancy, she had worked up her courage and made her request. And his answer hadn't been "no." At least, not outright.

He thought they needed to talk it over and although his insistence that they stay at his ranch had made her extremely nervous, she had agreed. She needed to reassure him that she would sign whatever document was needed to ensure that she would be solely responsible for the baby and that he would be under no obligation. She was sure that once he understood that, he would be more inclined to help her.

As she threw back the covers and got out of bed to take a shower, she thought about what Ryder would want to discuss first. He would probably start off with wanting to know why she didn't feel she would ever meet a man she wanted to marry. Or he might try to convince her that, at the youthful age of twenty-five, she had plenty of time and should wait to make such a life-changing decision.

Standing beneath the refreshing spray of warm water, she smiled. She might not have practiced the way she worded her request as much as she should have, but she was armed and ready with her answers for their upcoming discussion about it. She knew Ryder well enough to know he would try to talk her out of her plans, and she had painstakingly gone over the way she would explain her reasoning and how she would frame the responses she intended to give him. Once he realized that she was completely serious, along with the promise of a legal document relieving him of any commitment to support or help raise the child, surely he would agree.

Anxious to start their conversation, she toweled herself dry, quickly got dressed and started downstairs. Halfway to the bottom of the staircase, she stopped when she came face-to-face with one of the largest gray tabby cats she had ever seen.

"You must be Lucifer," she said tentatively. From Ryder's description of the cat, she wasn't sure how he would react to encountering a stranger in his domain.

She hoped he didn't attack her as she walked past. But instead of pouncing on her as she expected he might, the cat gazed up at her for a moment, then letting out a heartfelt meow, rubbed his body along the side of her leg.

Reaching down, she cautiously stroked his soft coat. Lucifer rewarded her with a loud, albeit contented purr. "You don't seem nearly as ferocious as Ryder claimed you were," she said when he burrowed his head into her palm, then licked her fingers with a swipe of his sandpapery rough tongue.

When Summer continued on down the stairs, Lucifer trotted behind her as she followed the delicious smell of fried bacon and freshly brewed coffee. "Good morning," she said when she found Ryder seated at the kitchen table.

"Morning." He rose from his chair as she entered the room, and Lucifer immediately arched his back and hissed loudly at Ryder. "I see he's still the same happy cat he's always been," Ryder said sarcastically as he shook his head. "Would you like a cup of coffee, Summer?"

"Yes, please. It smells wonderful."

"Just a little cream?" he asked. They had met for coffee so many times over the past few years, he knew exactly how she liked it. Just as she knew he always liked his coffee black.

"Yes, thank you." She smiled. "You know, I think Lucifer likes me. He rubbed against my leg and let me pet him when we met on the stairs."

"See, I told you it's just you he has a problem with, Ryder." The woman standing at the stove chortled.

"I don't know why." He looked as if he might be a bit insulted by her comment. "Most other animals don't seem to think I'm all that bad of a guy."

"Maybe you aren't home enough for him to get used to you," Summer suggested.

"Whatever." Shrugging, he walked over to take a mug from one of the top cabinets, then poured her some coffee. "Betty Lou Harmon, I'd like for you to meet my friend, Summer Patterson."

"It's nice to meet you, Mrs. Harmon," Summer said warmly as the older woman turned from the stove to face her.

"It's real nice to meet you, too, child. But don't go bein' all formal," the housekeeper groused, shaking her head. "You call me Betty Lou the same as everybody else, you hear?"

"Yes, ma'am," Summer said, instantly liking the woman. With her dark hair liberally streaked with silver and pulled back into a tight bun at the back of her head, her kind gray eyes and round cheeks flushed from the heat of the stove, Betty Lou looked more like someone's grandmother than a rancher's housekeeper.

Wiping her hands on her gingham apron, she waved toward the trestle table where Ryder had been seated when Summer entered the room. "You find yourself a place to sit and I'll get you fixed up with a plate of eggs, bacon, hash browns and some biscuits and gravy."

"I don't eat much for breakfast," Summer confessed, hoping she didn't offend the woman. She seated herself in one of the tall ladder-back chairs at the honey oak table. "Normally all I have is a bagel or toast and a cup of coffee."

"Well, you'd better eat a hearty meal this mornin' if you're goin' horseback ridin' down to the canyon with Ryder," Betty Lou said, filling a plate and bringing it over to set on the table in front of her.

"We're going for a ride?" Summer asked, crestfallen. She thought they were supposed to discuss her request.

"I thought I'd show you around the ranch," Ryder said, nodding as he brought her coffee over to the table. When Betty Lou went into the pantry, he lowered his voice and leaned close to Summer. "We'll have plenty of time to talk and no one around to overhear the conversation."

"We could have done that in my hotel room," she reminded him.

He raised one dark eyebrow as he sat back down at the head of the table. "For someone who is so concerned with appearances, you haven't thought of the obvious, darlin'."

Ryder's intimate tone and the scent of his clean, masculine skin caused her pulse to beat double time. "Wh-what would that be?" she asked, confused and not at all comfortable with the way she was reacting to him.

"How do you think it would look with us being alone in your room for several hours?" He shrugged. "I doubt anyone would be convinced we were just talking or watching television."

"Oh." She hadn't thought of that. "I suppose you're right."

"Now eat," he said, pointing to her plate.

"Aren't you going to have breakfast?" she asked, taking a bite of the fluffy scrambled eggs.

He took a sip of his coffee and shook his head. "I ate about an hour ago."

When she finished the last of the delicious food, Summer smiled at Betty Lou when she walked over to pick up the plate. "That was wonderful. Thank you."

The woman gave her an approving nod. "That should

tide you over until you eat the sandwiches I packed for the two of you."

"We won't be back in time for lunch?" Summer asked, turning to Ryder. "How far away is the canyon?"

"It's not that far." He gave her a smile that made her radiate from within. "But there's a creek lined with cottonwoods that runs through the canyon, and I thought you might like to have a picnic along the bank."

"I haven't done something like that in years," she said, happy that he had thought of the idea. Going on an outing like the one Ryder suggested was one of the many things she had enjoyed doing with her parents.

"You do know how to ride a horse, don't you?" he asked. When she nodded, he unclipped his cell phone from his belt. "Good. I'll call the barn and have my foreman get the horses saddled and ready for us."

A half hour later as he and Summer rode across the pasture behind the barns, Ryder watched her pat the buckskin mare she was riding. With the autumn sun shining down on her long blond hair, she looked like an angel. A very desirable angel.

He frowned at the thought. They had never been more than friends, and until his brothers started ribbing him about taking her to Sam and Bria's wedding vows renewal celebration, he had purposely avoided thinking of her in that way. So why was it all he could think about now? Of course, her making her plea last night for him to be her baby's daddy sure wasn't helping matters.

"I'm glad you thought of this, Ryder," she said, distracting him from his confusing inner thoughts. "I love going horseback riding. I used to do it all the time. But after I took the job with the rodeo association, I sold my parents' farm and all of the horses and I don't get to ride much anymore."

"Was there a reason you couldn't keep it?" he asked. She said she had plenty of money, so that couldn't be the cause of her selling everything.

She stared off into the distance like the decision might not have been an easy one to make. "With all the travel required for my job, it just didn't seem practical to hang on to it."

"I realize you have to arrive in a town a few days before a rodeo in order to get things set up for the media and schedule interviews for some of the riders, but couldn't you have boarded one of the horses and ridden on the days that you do make it home?" he asked, knowing that was what he would have done.

He could understand her not wanting to hold on to her parents' home without them being there. It would most likely be a painful reminder of all that she had lost when they were killed. But he didn't understand her not keeping at least one of the horses if she liked to ride that much.

"I don't go home," she answered, shrugging one slender shoulder. "I just go on to the next town on the schedule."

"You don't go back to your place on the few days we have off between rodeos?" They normally met up in the next town for the next rodeo and had never traveled together before. It appeared that although they were close friends, there was a lot that they hadn't shared with each other.

But he still couldn't imagine going for weeks without coming back to the ranch. Besides Hank Calvert's Last Chance Ranch, the Blue Canyon was the only place he had ever been able to truly call home. And a home of his own was something he never intended to be without again.

"I...don't have a place," she admitted, looking a little sheepish. "I know it sounds bad, but I couldn't see any sense in paying for the upkeep on my parents' home or rent on an apartment when I'd only be there a few days out of the month."

Reaching out, he took hold of the mare's reins as he stopped both horses. "Let me get this straight. You live out of hotel rooms and you don't have a place to call your own?" When she nodded, he asked, "Where do you keep your things?"

"What I can't pack into the two suitcases I take on the road with me, like furniture and family keepsakes, I keep in a storage unit in Topanga, California, not far from where my parents lived." When he turned loose of the buckskin's reins and they continued on toward the trail leading down into the canyon, she added, "It's much cheaper than paying to keep them in an apartment I'd never use."

Shocked by her revelation, he shook his head. "So for all intents and purposes, you're homeless."

"I guess it could be construed that way." She nibbled on her lower lip a moment as if she might be bothered by it more than she was letting on. "But as long as I'm traveling like I do, I don't mind."

"How long have you lived this way?" he asked, still trying to wrap his mind around what she had told him.

"About three years."

He had been friends with her all that time and not once had he suspected that she lived the life of a nomad. What else was there about her that he didn't know? And how the hell did she plan on taking care of a baby with that kind of lifestyle?

When they reached the canyon's rim, they fell silent as Ryder rode the bay ahead of her to lead the way to the meadow below. But he couldn't stop thinking about her lack of roots. Why did she want a baby when she didn't even have a home? What was she going to do with the poor little thing, raise it in a series of hotel rooms while they traveled from one rodeo to the next for her job? That wasn't any kind of a life for a little kid.

Ryder didn't know what her reasoning was, but he had every intention of finding out. He knew from personal experience that it was important to a kid to have a place to call home.

Leading the way to the spot along the bank that he had in mind for their picnic, he reined in the gelding. "How does this look?"

"It's great," she said, stopping the buckskin mare beside his horse. "There's plenty of shade." She pointed toward one of the cottonwoods. "And under that tree looks like the perfect place to put the blanket."

Dismounting the bay, he dropped the reins to ground-tie the horse, then moved to retrieve the rolled blanket he had tied to the back of the gelding's saddle, along with the insulated saddlebags holding their lunch. From the corner of his eye, he watched Summer jump down from the mare's back and start doing some stretches to loosen up after the ride.

He briefly wondered if she was having muscle cramps, but he quickly forgot all about her possible discomfort as he watched her stretch from side to side, then bend over to touch her toes. Her jeans pulled tight over her perfect little bottom caused his mouth to go as dry as a desert in a drought. When she straightened, then placed her hands on her hips to lean back and relieve pressure on her lower back, he sucked in a sharp breath. Her motions caused her chest to stick out and for the first time since he had known her, he noticed how full and perfect her breasts were.

Ryder muttered a curse under his breath and forced himself to look away. This was Summer. She was his best friend and he'd never thought of her in a romantic light. So why now was he suddenly taking notice of her delightful backside and enticing breasts?

Disgusted with himself, he shook his head and tucking the picnic blanket under his arm, finished unfastening the insulated saddlebags from the bay's saddle and carted everything over to the spot beneath the cottonwood that Summer had pointed out. His fascination with her feminine attributes was probably due to the fact that he hadn't been with a woman in longer than he cared to remember—and he'd have to be blind not to notice that Summer was a damned good-looking woman with a set of curves that could tempt a eunuch. He wasn't at all comfortable thinking of her in that way, but there was no denying it either.

As he set the saddlebags down and unfolded the blanket to spread it out on the ground, he gave some thought to his dilemma. He was a normal, healthy adult male who, like any other man, needed to occasionally get lost in a woman's softness. Once he got back out on the rodeo circuit, he needed to take a trip to one of the local watering holes in whatever town he was in and strike up a cozy little acquaintance with a woman who wasn't looking for anything more than a real good time. Maybe then he would stop having inappropriate thoughts about his best friend.

Three

Sitting beside the lazy little creek after finishing their lunch, Summer glanced over at Ryder's handsome profile. He really was one of the best-looking men she had ever known and she had a hard time believing it took her this long to realize it. Studying his features, she found herself hoping that if he agreed to help her, their child would look like him. But neither of them had brought up the subject of her request and the longer it took for them to start the discussion, the more uncertain she became. What if he refused to be the sperm donor?

He had all the attributes she wanted for her child and asking any of the other men she knew wasn't even a consideration. She didn't know them well enough to determine if they had the traits she was looking for, and truthfully, she didn't want to get that well acquainted with them. She didn't trust any man the way she trusted

Ryder and couldn't imagine anyone else as her baby's father.

"Have you given any more thought to helping me?" she finally asked.

"I really haven't thought about much of anything else," he admitted, turning to face her. "It's not every day that out of the clear blue sky a woman asks me to help her get pregnant." His expression gave nothing away and she had no indication of what he might be thinking.

"As I told you last night, you wouldn't be obligated in any way," she said, hoping to reassure him. "I'll be responsible for everything. You wouldn't even have to acknowledge that you were the donor."

"In other words, you don't want me to be involved at all in my own kid's life," he said flatly. Shaking his head, he added, "You of all people should know that's not the way I roll, darlin'."

The steely determination she heard in his voice surprised her. "I…well…I hadn't thought you would want—"

He held up his hand. "Let's back up. We can cover what would happen after you became pregnant a little later on. Right now, I have a few things I'd like to know."

"Of course," she said pleasantly. She was confident she could answer all of his questions. "What would you like to ask first?"

Ryder's piercing green gaze held her captive. "Why me?"

"You have all the qualities that I would want passed

on to my child," she said, not having to think about her answer. "You're healthy, physically fit, as well as physically appealing. You're also honest, loyal and other than my late father, you're the most trustworthy man I've ever known."

"You make me sound like a prize stud someone would want to cover their herd of mares," he said, shaking his head in obvious disbelief. "How long have you been thinking about this?"

"About six months," she admitted. Things weren't going the way she had hoped. He didn't sound as if he was all that receptive to the idea. "But I didn't seriously think of approaching you until a couple of weeks ago."

Nodding as if he accepted her answer, Ryder stared off into space for a moment before he asked, "Last night you told me you didn't want to wait to see if you change your mind about meeting a man you might want to settle down with."

"That's right." She shook her head. "I don't have any intention of ever getting married."

"Why?"

"As you know, I'm pretty independent," she said, reciting the answer she had rehearsed. "I don't want to lose that. I don't want to be dependent on a man or give anyone that kind of control over me."

He frowned. "Where did you get the idea that whoever you met would want to control you?" Shaking his head, he propped his forearms on his bent knees. "Most men I know admire independence in a woman. Me included."

"Maybe I should rephrase that," she said, thinking

quickly. “I don’t want to give that kind of emotional control to anyone.”

Staring at her for several long moments, Ryder asked, “Who was the bastard?”

His question startled her. “I…don’t know what you mean.”

“Someone had to have hurt you pretty bad to make you feel this way,” he insisted. “Who was he?”

Ryder’s assessment was hitting too close to the truth and she had to force herself to remain calm. “There wasn’t anyone,” she lied. “I’ve just never believed that I need a man in my life to validate my worth as a woman nor do I want to depend on him for my happiness.”

“Okay,” he said slowly. She could tell he wasn’t buying her explanation, but before she had the chance to say more, he asked, “Why now? You’re only twenty-five. It’s not like your biological clock is ticking or the alarm is about to go off.”

She took a deep breath. Her answer this time wasn’t a lie or a half-truth. “I want to be part of a family again, Ryder. I want someone to love and be loved by in return.”

“Ah, darlin’,” he said, moving to wrap his strong arms around her. Pulling her to him, he gave her a comforting hug. “I know how alone you’ve been since your parents passed away, but do you really think having a baby will be the cure for your loneliness?”

“I really do,” she said, feeling a bit confused by the fact that Ryder’s embrace wasn’t the least bit intimidating. Any other man giving her a hug would have sent her into a panic attack.

"What would you do about a home for you and the baby?" he asked, his tone gentle. "You can't raise a kid living in hotel rooms and moving from town to town every week."

His questions had her wondering if he might be seriously considering her request. "I intend to quit my job and buy a house. As I told you before, my parents left me quite well-off. Between their life insurance policies and the sale of the horses and ranch, I never have to work another day in my life if I don't want to." She exhaled slowly. "I'd like to be a stay-at-home mom until my baby is old enough for preschool. Then after my child starts school, I'll decide whether I want to find something to do part-time or continue being a stay-at-home mom." When Ryder remained silent, she leaned back to look at him. He appeared to be in deep thought and she hoped that was a positive sign he was going to help her.

"This is a big decision," he finally said, meeting her questioning gaze. "Let me think about it for a while."

"Of course," she said slowly. "But let me assure you, I don't expect you to do anything past being the donor. Like I said last night…you won't be obligated in any way for anything."

He continued to stare at her for what seemed like an eternity, then he rose to his feet and held out his hand to help her to hers. "I think it's about time we head back to the house."

When she placed her hand in his, a jolt of electric current streaked up her arm and spread throughout her insides. Summer frowned at the lingering sensation as she turned to pick up the blanket. What was going on with her? She wasn't interested in any man and especially not Ryder. He was her best friend and even if she had wanted to have a man in her life—which she didn't—she wasn't willing to jeopardize their friendship by starting something romantic. Sperm donation was one thing, involving emotions was another.

But as they rode back toward the ranch house, she couldn't stop thinking about the unsettling feeling that had coursed through her. Why was she suddenly more aware of Ryder as a man than ever before? And why, when he took her hand in his, did it feel as if something extremely significant had shifted in the universe?

While Summer helped Betty Lou finish up supper in the kitchen, Ryder stood by the window in his office, staring out at the sun sinking low in the western sky. He couldn't stop thinking about Summer's misguided idea that a baby was the solution to her loneliness.

It wasn't that he couldn't understand her wanting a family connection and the sense of belonging that came with it. He could. For the first fourteen years of his life, he had longed for the same thing as he was shuffled from one foster home to another. It wasn't until he was placed in the care of Hank Calvert and taken to live at the Last Chance Ranch that he learned what it felt like to have a home and be part of a family. But he was doubtful that her having a baby would make her feel like she was part of something like that again.

Normally, having a family meant having a built-in support system. But Summer wouldn't have that.

She would be the support system for the baby, but she wouldn't have anyone to help her. Who would be there to lend a hand with a fussy newborn when she got so tired she was about to drop in her tracks? Who would she lean on if, God forbid, the baby came down with a serious illness? That role was usually filled by a husband, a woman's mother or even her sister. Summer wouldn't have any of the three.

He wasn't buying into her claim that fearing the loss of her independence was the reason behind her not wanting to have a man in her life either. She had to know that in this day and time, most men were fine with a woman being strong and self-assured. And that wasn't the only thing that bothered him about their conversation.

Why did she believe that he wouldn't want to be part of his own kid's life? What made her think that if he lost what little sense he had and agreed to father her baby that he could just walk away?

He knew firsthand the effect a parent's abandonment had on a kid. He might have only been four years old when his mother left him in a hospital waiting room for the authorities to find, but her poor choice had a huge impact on his life. Aside from being raised by people who didn't care anything about him past the monthly check they received for housing him, the fallout of being shuffled from one unsuitable family to another had eventually landed him in enough trouble to be sent to the Last Chance Ranch. And although becoming one of Hank's boys had been the best thing that ever happened to him, the way he got there was something nobody would want for a kid.

Of course, Summer wasn't asking him to bond with the child and then leave to let her finish raising him or her. She didn't want him to be part of the baby's life at all. And that bothered the hell out of him.

Until Summer made her request, he had never given a lot of thought to having a child of his own. For one thing, he hadn't ever expected to get married. Finding a woman who understood his painful past and could overlook all that would be a tall order to fill. And for another, thanks to Hank's Cowboy Code, Ryder was old-fashioned enough to believe that you weren't supposed to put the cart before the horse. Getting married was what a man was supposed to do first, then start having kids. Not the other way around.

He couldn't help but smile fondly at the memory of his foster father sitting Ryder and the rest of his brothers down for lessons in manners and morality. Whether it was out of gratitude or they all wanted to emulate the man who had been there for them through thick and thin, Ryder and his brothers had learned their lessons well. A man always treated a woman like a lady, showed her respect and if he fathered a child, he owned up to his responsibility and helped the mother raise it.

He and his brothers all adhered to the Cowboy Code to this day—even Nate. He might be a ladies' man, but he was always respectful of women and limited his amorous activities to one woman at a time.

A knock on the door interrupted his thoughts. "Dinner is almost ready, Ryder," Summer called out to him.

Walking over to open the door, his heart stalled at the sight of her. With strands of her honey-blond hair escaping the confines of her ponytail and her cheeks colored a pretty pink from the heat of cooking, he didn't think he had ever seen her look lovelier.

"Lead the way," he said, wondering if he'd lost his mind. Why did he feel as if he had just run a footrace? Hell, he didn't get this out of breath when he played chicken with a ton of pissed-off beef.

As he watched her walk down the hall ahead of him, Ryder couldn't seem to stop watching the enticing sway of her hips. He gritted his teeth and forced himself to focus on the back of her head. Why, in the past couple of days, had he suddenly become so fascinated with her body?

He wouldn't even begin to entertain the idea of having something develop between them. For that matter, he wasn't willing to become romantically involved with *any* woman. He just couldn't bear the thought of falling for someone special and then seeing the revulsion and fear on her face once she learned the truth about him.

Entering the kitchen, he started toward his place at the head of the table, but Lucifer chose that moment to walk out from behind the kitchen island. As was his usual practice whenever he saw Ryder, the cat arched its back and let loose with a nasty hiss.

"Well, good evening to you, too, Lucifer," Ryder said cheerfully. He would have never believed he would be glad to cross paths with the disagreeable feline, but it had been just the distraction he needed to get his mind off Summer's shapely bottom.

"There's something about you that cat doesn't like," Summer said, crinkling her brow. "Maybe he's sensitive to your cologne."

Ryder shrugged as he sat down at the table. "He might be if I wore cologne. But since I don't, it can't be that."

"Do you have any idea why Lucifer reacts to Ryder the way he does, Betty Lou?" she asked, picking up a bowl of mashed potatoes from the island to set it on the table.

The older woman shook her head. "No, but he's been this way about Ryder ever since I started housekeepin' here four years ago." She walked over to place a platter of country fried steaks in the middle of the table. "I personally think Lucifer is bein' defensive because he's intimidated by Ryder's size." She grinned. "You gotta admit, Ryder's a long, tall drink of water."

"You might be right." Summer smiled as she poured them all glasses of iced tea. "Maybe Lucifer is just warning Ryder to look down and not step on him."

While the two women continued to speculate on why the cat found him so offensive, Ryder's thoughts turned to what he needed to say to change Summer's mind about pursuing her quest to get pregnant. Knowing her the way he did, he needed to be careful not to argue too strongly against her plans. If he did that, she just might end up more determined than ever to proceed with or without his help.

As an idea began to take shape, he waited until Betty Lou turned her attention to getting a pie out of the oven before he motioned Summer over to the table. "I've come to a decision," he said, careful to keep his tone low. "If you aren't too tired, we'll talk about it in my office after we eat."

An hour after Ryder told her he was ready to give her his answer, Summer followed him down the hall to his office. She didn't think she had ever been more nervous than she was at that moment. What if his answer was "no"? What would she do then?

When they walked into the thoroughly masculine room, he motioned toward the big leather armchair in front of his desk as he closed the door behind them. "Have a seat."

Lowering himself into the plush executive chair behind his big walnut desk, Ryder's smile gave her more hope than she'd had since making her request. "Before I agree, I think there are a few details that we need to discuss further."

"You're going to help me?" Her heart soared and unable to sit still she leaned forward. "Thank you, Ryder. You have no idea how much this means to me!"

He held up his hand as he shook his head. "I didn't say that, Summer. I said there would be things we would need to talk over before I agreed to anything."

"I thought I was pretty clear about my plans and your role in them." She had gone over everything so many times in her head, she couldn't think of anything she might have left out.

"You were very clear," he concurred. "But there are a few things that I would want in return for my donation to this cause of yours."

"What would that be?" she asked cautiously.

"You know all about my mother abandoning me when I was four years old and that I spent the rest of my childhood in the foster care system." When she nodded, he went on, "But I don't think I ever told you that I never knew who my father was." He shrugged. "For that matter, I doubt my mother did, either."

"What makes you think she didn't know your father?" Summer asked. "You were so little, maybe you just forgot her mentioning him."

"I don't think so." Shaking his head, Ryder sat back in his chair. "From what one of my caseworkers said just before I was sent to the Last Chance Ranch, my mother had been on their radar practically from the time I was born. Apparently at some point in their investigations, she had told the authorities she wasn't sure who had made her pregnant."

"I'm sorry, Ryder," she said softly. Having had a wonderful childhood with two loving parents, she couldn't imagine not having that security or the sense of identity that came with it. "But what does that have to do with you helping me?"

"I spent the first fourteen years of my life wondering who my father was and wishing that I had a dad to do things with like the other kids I went to school with. It wasn't until Hank Calvert became my foster father that I learned what it was like to have a real dad." He sat forward and placing his forearms on the desk, loosely clasped his hands in front of him. "If I agreed to father your child, I wouldn't want my kid going through that. I don't want him growing up wondering who's responsible for his existence and why his dad isn't around to take him places and do things with him."

"Are you telling me you want to be part of the baby's life?" She had been so busy assuring him that he wouldn't be obligated in any way that she hadn't considered Ryder might actually want the responsibility of helping her raise the child.

"Who knows? This might be the only kid I ever have," he answered. "But whether it is or not, I would want to be there for him or her like my biological father never was for me."

As Summer thought about what he said, she remembered the relationship she had with her father and how much it had meant to both of them. She had so many wonderful memories of things they had done together that she realized she wanted that for her child, as well.

"I would really like for you to be a part of the baby's life," she said, meaning it. She knew Ryder well enough to know that he would be a great father. "I just hadn't considered that you might want to be."

"Would you be agreeable to joint custody?" he asked, looking as if he thought his request might be a deal breaker.

"I haven't given it any thought," she answered truthfully. "But as long as we talk and agree on how to raise the baby, I don't think I would have a problem with it."

He raised one dark eyebrow. "You do realize that I would want equal time with him or her, don't you?"

"I'm sure we could work out something that we both find acceptable." They were best friends and got along quite well, so it shouldn't be that hard to arrange a suitable schedule. "Is that all?"

"No." He met her questioning gaze. "Where were you thinking about buying that house you mentioned?"

"I hadn't thought that far ahead, but I suppose I could buy a home anywhere," she said. With her parents gone and their property sold, there was no longer anything for her in California. "Why?"

Instead of answering her, he asked, "Would you be open to staying here at the ranch while you're pregnant and up until the baby is a year old, then finding a place close by?"

"I'm not sure that's a good idea, Ryder," she said, wondering how her simple request had suddenly become so complex. The longer they talked, the more complicated things became and the more concessions she was having to make.

"Actually, it's the perfect solution," he persisted. "If you stayed here at the ranch, I could experience the pregnancy with you, as well as go to your doctor appointments and whatever prenatal classes we need to take to get ready to become parents. Then once the baby is born, I could help out with its care during the first year. And when the time comes for you to find a house, being close by would make sharing custody a lot easier."

What he said made sense, but she wasn't ready to agree without giving it more thought. They might be best friends, but she wasn't sure she wanted to live with him for the better part of two years.

"Could I think about all of this for a little while?" she finally asked.

He smiled. "Sure. Take your time."

"Is there anything else?" Surely they had covered everything.

Ryder paused for a moment, then continued, "There's just one more thing..."

"I'm listening," she said, wondering what on earth there was left for him to ask of her before he agreed to help her.

"I don't think my making a donation in a cup is the route we should take for the conception." He shook his head. "I've got all the right equipment and trust me, darlin', everything is completely operational," he said, grinning. "Besides, I'd like to be able to tell our kid that we purposely got together because we both wanted him or her."

A knot started to form in the pit of her stomach. "Wh-what are you trying to say, Ryder?"

"If I'm going to help you, the conception would have to be natural."

"You mean, we would—"

"Make love," he finished for her.

"No!" Even she was startled by the vehemence in her one word answer. But there was absolutely no way she was going to bed with any man and especially not Ryder. He was her friend and she didn't want to lose their relationship.

"Then I guess the deal is off," he said, leaning back in his chair.

"Is there anything I can say to change your mind?"

she asked, knowing from his expression that it was unlikely she could convince him to see reason.

"No." He shook his head. "As far as I'm concerned, the means of conception is nonnegotiable."

She stood up to leave. "Then please forget that I asked for your help."

"I can't do that, darlin'." He shook his head as he rose to his feet. "That horse is already out of the barn and there's no way to get it back."

Staring at him a moment, Summer shook her head and hurried out of Ryder's office. As she marched up the stairs to the bedroom she had used since her arrival the night before, several emotions coursed through her. Naturally, she was disappointed. She wanted a baby and she wanted Ryder to father him or her. She was also a bit embarrassed that she'd had such a strong reaction to the idea of their having sex. He had no way of knowing that the very idea of having sex with any man came close to sending her into a panic attack. But more than that, she was angry.

As she'd stood in his office, staring at him as she tried to think of something to make him change his mind, it had occurred to her that she was the one having to make all of the concessions. It was true that most of what he had asked of her made sense. Given that he had never known his father, she could understand why he didn't want that for his child and even admired him for his willingness to be committed to being there for the baby.

But couldn't he at least consider her feelings on the matter? Why wasn't he willing to compromise on how the baby was conceived? Didn't he realize how far over the line that would be taking their friendship? Hadn't he considered that their relationship might not survive their being intimate?

A shiver ran through her and to her dismay it wasn't one of apprehension or panic. She frowned. Surely the unfamiliar sensation wasn't anticipation.

Shaking her head at the foolish thought, she grabbed her pajamas and headed into the bathroom for a quick shower. She needed to think of a way to get him to see reason. Unfortunately, all that kept running through her mind was the idea that Ryder was the only man she would even come close to considering making a baby with the old-fashioned way.

After Summer left his office like the hounds of hell chased her, Ryder sighed heavily and sank back down in his chair behind the desk as he thought about what had taken place. He had accomplished what he set out to do. He had successfully discouraged her from wanting him to father her child. So why didn't he feel good about it?

He hadn't wanted to crush her dream, but he honestly believed she wanted to have a child for the wrong reason. Having a baby simply because she wanted a connection with family again would be putting a lot of expectations on a kid that might prove hard for him or her to live up to.

Of course Summer would love the baby and the kid would love her. Ryder had no doubt about that. But he was of the opinion that a child should be wanted because of a desire to nurture and cherish it, not to be a remedy for loneliness.

But as much as her misguided reason for wanting a baby bothered him, something else bothered him more. What had caused her reaction when he mentioned conceiving a child the old-fashioned way?

Over the course of their friendship, he had seen her in several stressful situations and one of the many things he admired about Summer was her ability to remain calm and self-assured. She could handle a pressroom full of demanding reporters as easily as she applied her makeup. And last year, when one of the young bull riders had died from injuries sustained at one of the rodeos, she had immediately taken charge and somehow managed to keep the media satisfied without them hounding the family while they mourned the loss of their only son.

But he didn't think he had ever seen her thrown off balance the way she had been when he mentioned conceiving a baby by making love. Her confidence seemed to disappear before his eyes and a hesitancy that he would have never expected came over her.

Ryder scowled. Was the thought of making love with him that unpleasant? Or was she afraid of losing the comfortable friendship they had shared for the past several years?

Although he wasn't overly proud of himself for feeling the way he did, a small part of him had actually hoped she would agree to his terms. He had originally thought of his plan as a deterrent—a way to get her to give up on her idea that she wanted him to be her baby daddy. But just the thought of holding Summer's delightful body against his, of burying himself deep inside of her, caused the region south of his belt buckle to harden so fast it made him feel light-headed.

"McClain, you're one miserable son of a bitch," he muttered, rising from his chair and starting toward the office door.

Summer was his best friend, and for the life of him, he couldn't figure out what had changed between them over the past twenty-four hours that kept him in a state of semiarousal. He would like to blame his sudden unwarranted lust on her proposing the idea of him fathering her child. But he couldn't. Her hands on his biceps when they danced at the party had charged him up like the toy rabbit in one of those battery commercials—and that had been hours before she had asked him to help her become pregnant. And he had given up on blaming his brothers' teasing him about her as having any bearing on the situation at all. Hell, they had ribbed him countless times over the past several years about his relationship with her and not once had he started wondering what it would be like to sink himself so deep inside of her that he lost track of where he ended and she began.

His traitorous body tightened further and he made a beeline for the master bathroom and a cold shower. Maybe if he stood beneath the icy spray until he was colder than a penguin's tail feathers on an arctic ice floe, he would once again start thinking of Summer as his friend and stop thinking of her as the desirable woman who wanted him to help her make a baby.

Long after she heard Ryder walk past her room on his way to the master suite, Summer lay in bed staring at the ceiling. She couldn't stop thinking about what he said and how she had reacted to it.

She had been fine with almost all of his requirements. In fact, she decided that she liked the idea of sharing the responsibilities of raising their child with him. As protective as he was of those he cared for and as patient as she knew him to be, he would have been a great father. And she could understand him wanting her to live at the ranch with him during her pregnancy and for the baby's first year, too. He intended to be an involved father—going to doctor appointments and attending childbirth classes, as well as taking his turn at caring for the baby once it was born. She could even appreciate him wanting her to buy a home close to the ranch so that he could be with their child as often as possible. But his idea that they needed to conceive their child naturally was completely out of her comfort zone.

Shivering, she turned to her side and scrunching her eyes shut, she tried to block out the ugly memory behind her intimacy issues. She didn't like thinking about that night and the man who had violated her body and destroyed her trust in men. It gave him and the incident too much importance—too much power over her. Unfortunately, it had become a significant detail of her past and one that had shaped her future, as well as all of her future relationships with other men. At least all of them, that is, but her friendship with Ryder.

From the moment she met him, she had trusted Ryder. She wasn't sure why, but for some reason she had known he was everything he appeared to be—open, honest and respectful of women. The type of man her father had been. The type of man all men should be.

But as much as she wanted a baby, having sex with Ryder—a man she trusted more than any other—was something she just wasn't certain she could do. For one thing, she had avoided putting herself in a vulnerable situation with a man for so long that she wasn't sure she could do it again. And for another, up until the night she was raped, she had only been with one other man. That had been her freshman year in college, and although having sex with her boyfriend had been all right, their few times together certainly hadn't lived up to her expectations or sounded anything like the passionate encounters her roommate had talked about having with her boyfriend.

Turning to her back again, Summer opened her eyes to stare at the ceiling. She still wanted a child and it looked as if a sperm bank would be her only option. But did she really want to visit one in order to get the baby she wanted?

The thought still turned her off big-time. What if she couldn't find a donor that would be an acceptable substitute for Ryder? Or worse yet, what if she did and the guy lied about his medical history or his characteristics?

She knew there was a screening process that men went through before they were allowed to donate and that did give her some small amount of comfort. But the bottom line was—her baby would be fathered by a total stranger and that was something that made her extremely uneasy.

Upset by the idea of having to visit a sperm bank

and unable to sleep, Summer threw back the covers and got out of bed to walk over to the window seat. Sinking down onto the plush cushion, she drew her legs up to her chest and wrapped her arms around them as she stared out the window at the star-studded night sky. There was only one man she wanted to father her child and that was Ryder McClain.

Now that she knew that no other man would be an acceptable substitute, she had to decide if she could work up the courage to go through with his condition that the conception be natural. It would mean having sex with him, and even though it would only be for the purpose of becoming pregnant, she just wasn't sure she would be able to do it.

The thought caused an empty ache to begin to pool in her lower belly and she quickly stood up to pace the room. It had been so long since she experienced the sensation, she had almost forgotten what it felt like. But there was no mistaking it. Her mind might not be able to come to terms with his demand, but her body was more than ready.

Walking into the bathroom, she bent over the sink, turned on the cold water and splashed some on her face. Ryder was her friend, the only male she felt completely at ease spending time with. As she patted her face dry with a towel, she raised her eyes to meet the gaze of her image in the mirror. And although she wasn't the least bit comfortable with it, he was the only man who had made her feel the stirrings of desire in several years.

Four

The next morning as he brushed the shiny coat of his bay gelding, Ryder couldn't help but wonder if he had done irreparable damage to his friendship with Summer. He hoped with all his heart that wasn't the case.

When he suggested they make love in order for her to conceive, he had only meant to discourage her, not have her running for the hills. But he hadn't seen her since their conversation in his study yesterday evening and she hadn't even bothered coming downstairs for breakfast this morning. But for the life of him, he couldn't think of any other explanation for her absence.

He hadn't expected her to accept his terms and thanks to the ice-cold shower he had taken, his perspective had been restored. Although he realized her refusal had been for the best, he hadn't counted on his demands alienating her. The fact that she was avoiding him was testament to the fact that they probably had and it bothered him. A lot.

"Betty Lou said I'd probably find you here," Summer said, surprising him when she walked into the barn.

"I wasn't entirely sure you would ever talk to me again after our discussion last night," he said honestly. "You didn't join me for breakfast and I figured you were still pretty upset with me over our talk."

He continued brushing the bay to keep from giving in to the overwhelming urge to take her into his arms. That made no sense at all and he couldn't figure out why the feeling was so strong. Theirs had never been that kind of friendship.

She shook her head. "I'm not upset, but you did give me a lot to think about and I had a hard time going to sleep."

"So you overslept this morning?" he asked, relieved she wasn't mad at him, but wondering where the conversation was going.

Nodding, a frown wrinkled her forehead. "I haven't slept that late in years."

"You probably needed the rest." He unsnapped the lead rope he had used to tie his horse to the grooming post and taking hold of the halter, walked the bay gelding back into the stall. Closing the half door, he added, "I've seen you work some pretty crazy hours lately." A slight breeze blew a strand of her blond hair across her cheek and it took monumental effort on his part not to reach out and brush it aside.

"If you aren't too busy, do you mind if we talk a bit

more about last night?" she asked, sounding a little unsure.

His heart slammed against his ribs and the back of his neck tingled with apprehension. What could she want to talk about that they hadn't covered last night? And why did he suddenly want to wrap his arms around her and kiss away the uncertain expression on her pretty face?

Instead, he swallowed around the cotton coating his throat and nodded. "Sure. Would you like to go back up to the house or do you want to talk here?" When she looked around as if checking to see if they were alone, he added, "Don't worry. There's no one around to overhear what we say. My foreman took the men out to check the fences in the far pastures to make sure they're ready for winter."

"Here will be fine," she said as she walked over to sit down on a bale of straw.

He was happy that she was at least still speaking to him, but mystified about what she thought they needed to discuss further. As far as he was concerned, his stipulations had been quite clear and set in stone. She wasn't going to convince him to change his mind.

"What do you think we need to discuss?" he asked, crossing his arms and leaning back against the bay's stall across the wide barn aisle from her.

She took a deep breath. "I spent the majority of last night lying awake, thinking about your requirements and your reasoning behind them."

"And?"

"I agree with most of them." She picked up a piece

of straw and staring down at it began to shred it with her fingers. "I like the idea of the baby having two parents who will love and be there for it. And I also think it would be nice to have you go with me to doctor appointments and help with the baby's care once it's born."

He wondered when she was going to stop beating around the bush and get to the sticking point—the part about them making love in order for her to conceive. He didn't have long to wait.

"The only problem I had with your requests was the part about us having sex to make me pregnant," she said, her voice almost a whisper.

"I understand your refusal and I'm not in the least bit offended, darlin'," he answered. "You don't want to risk our friendship and I'm fine with that. I don't want to lose it either."

His breath lodged in his lungs when she shook her head. "That isn't what I was about to tell you."

Clearing his suddenly rusty throat, he asked, "What were you going to say?"

"I've thought a lot about it...and I believe our friendship is solid enough to withstand our having sexual intercourse for the purpose of conceiving a child."

It was the last thing he'd expected her to say, and he wasn't at all comfortable with his body's reaction at her mention of them making love. Just the thought sent a shaft of longing coursing through him at the speed of light and caused his body to tighten predictably. Removing his hat, he lowered it in front of him with one hand as he ran his other hand through his hair in an effort to hide his reaction to what she had just said.

Hell's bells! He thought he had a handle on things and the matter had been settled. Last night, he'd told her what he wanted in return for helping her get pregnant and she had found his demands unacceptable. That should have been the end of it. When had he lost control of the situation? And what the hell was he going to do about it now?

"You want a baby so much that you're willing to take that step?" he asked, still unable to believe what she had told him. "You're willing to make love with me until you become pregnant?"

She closed her eyes a moment, then nodding, she met his gaze head-on. "Yes. I'm willing to do whatever I have to do in order to have the baby I want."

"Okay," he said slowly. "Can I ask why you changed your mind?"

There was no hesitation when she nodded. "You have all the traits and characteristics—"

"Yeah, I'm the prize stud," he interrupted. "I got that before. What I want to know is what happened to change your mind between last night and now?"

"I realized that you're the only man I want to father my baby." She shrugged one slender shoulder. "You're my best friend and I know you well enough to safely say that you'll be there for the baby no matter what. You'll love the child as much as I will and protect him or her from all harm."

He couldn't argue with her assessment of how he would feel about a kid. There wasn't a doubt in his mind that he would willingly lay down his life if that's what it took to keep it safe. For that matter, he would do the same for Summer.

"And you're completely comfortable with all this?" he asked, feeling like he might be lost somewhere in a parallel universe.

"Yes."

Ryder nodded as he stared off into space. Now what was he supposed to do? His plan had been to discourage her and it had been successful—last night. But now that Summer had changed her mind, he was trapped. He had given her his word that he would help her if she agreed to his terms and short of going back on it, he didn't see any other option but to honor his end of the bargain.

"I guess now all there is left to do is decide when you want to start trying to become pregnant," he finally said, clenching his fist into a tight ball in an effort to control his rapidly hardening body. Unfortunately, it wasn't working.

Squaring her shoulders, she rose to her feet. "I've given that some thought as well and I'd like to get started as soon as possible." Her cheeks colored a pretty pink. "We could start trying sometime today if that's all right with you."

It was all he could do not to groan aloud. A beautiful woman was standing in front of him, telling him that she wanted him to make love to her, and he was going to turn her down? His nobility only went so far and he was man enough to admit that he had reached the end of his.

"Sure," he said thickly as he pushed away from the bay's stall. Just the thought that they were going to make love sent a wave of heat straight to his groin, and he was glad she was too distracted to notice he was still holding his hat in front of jeans that were becoming way too snug at the fly. "I have some chores I have to take care of today, but this evening will be fine."

She nodded as she started to leave. "Now that things are settled, I'll go see if Betty Lou needs help with lunch." Stopping suddenly, she turned back. "By the way, do you wear boxers or briefs?"

"Boxer briefs." He frowned. "Why?"

"I'm not sure about those," she said, nibbling on her lower lip. "Until we're successful, you might want to start wearing boxers."

"Why?" Ryder knew he sounded like a damned parrot, but he couldn't figure out why she was so fixated on the type of underwear he preferred.

"Boxer shorts are less confining and enable more sperm production," she explained.

He laughed, releasing some of the tension that gripped him. "Don't worry about me, darlin'. Everything is in working order and since I sleep in the buff, I have no reason to believe that I won't have more than enough swimmers to get the job done."

"All right," she said as she turned to leave. "I'll trust that detail to you."

When she walked out of the barn, his smile faded and the reality of the situation set in. He and Summer were going to cross a line in their friendship and make love to have a baby. Un-freaking-believable!

If someone had told him three days ago that he would be consciously planning to make any woman pregnant, he would have laughed them right into the next county. But if they had told him that woman would be Summer Patterson, he would have readily told them that they were a few beers shy of a six-pack in the brains department.

A sudden thought had him cussing a blue streak as he jammed his hat back on his head. What were his brothers going to say when they found out about his arrangement with Summer?

He had no doubt that he would have their full support in whatever he did. But it would come with a pretty hefty price tag. Ryder knew as surely as the sun rose in the east each morning that he would have to endure endless ribbing and enough *I told you so's* to last a lifetime.

Picking up the brush he had used on the bay, he headed down the aisle toward the stalls at the end of the barn. His brothers' comments and jokes were just something he would have to cowboy up and deal with. As Hank always told him and his brothers, a man is only as good as his word and it should be as binding as any written contract.

Ryder tied the buckskin mare to the side of the stall and began brushing her dark golden coat. He felt like he was about to jump off a cliff into an unknown abyss, but he had made a promise to Summer and he would climb a barbed-wire fence buck naked before he reneged on it now.

After dinner, Summer helped Betty Lou clean up the kitchen, then slowly walked down the hall to join Ryder in the family room. She was as jittery as she could ever remember being, but she was determined to carry through with her plan. It meant too much to her to let anything stand in her way of having the family she wanted.

"Would you like to see a movie before we head upstairs to bed?" he asked, looking up from the show he had been watching when she entered the room. "There's a comedy you might like on one of the movie channels."

"I...um, no, I don't think so," she said, shaking her head. She'd had the entire day to think about what they were going to do and delaying it further would only increase her anxiety and could very well cause her to lose her nerve. She looked over her shoulder toward the kitchen to make sure Betty Lou had gone to her room. "If you don't mind, I'd just as soon go ahead and get started on our...little project."

He gave a short nod, then picking up the remote control, turned off the television and rose to his feet. "I went ahead and turned down the bed," he said, walking over to her. He paused for a moment before he reached up to touch her cheek with his forefinger. "Darlin', are you 100 percent sure this is what you really want to do?"

"Yes," she said as she fixed her attention on one of the snap closures on his chambray shirt. "Why do you ask?"

"Because you look like you're about to face a firing squad instead of going upstairs to make love with me," he said, frowning. He used his index finger to lift her chin until their gazes met. "You know it's okay if you've changed your mind. I'll understand and we'll go along like nothing ever happened."

The sincerity in his dark green eyes indicated that he really meant every word he said.

"No, I haven't changed my mind," she said decisively. "I just want to get this part over with so I can concentrate on looking forward to when the baby arrives."

His frown deepened as he placed his hand to her back and they walked over to the stairs. "You make it sound like you think making love with me is going to be about as pleasant as getting a tooth pulled."

"Not at all," she lied. "I'm just a little nervous. That's all." That was an understatement, she thought when they reached the top of the stairs and started down the hall. He might stir long dormant desires, but the thought of being intimate with any man was still extremely intimidating.

When she stopped to open the door to the bedroom she had been using, he shook his head. "I think it would be better if we go to my room."

A chilling trepidation streaked up her spine. "Why?"

He smiled encouragingly. "Betty Lou's room downstairs is on this side of the house, and I thought that you might not be overly comfortable with that."

"You're probably right," she said, forcing herself to continue on to the master suite at the end of the hall.

When they entered his bedroom and he turned on a lamp, she tried not to focus on the king-size bed and looked around at the Western decor. A blend of Native American artwork and Western wildlife prints graced the sage-colored walls, while colorful Navajo rugs brightened up the dark hardwood floor. The room was beautiful and perfect for Ryder. He was a Texas cowboy from the top of his dark brown hair to the soles of his big, booted feet and the room reflected that.

"Relax," he said, turning to face her. He reached out and put his arms loosely around her waist. "Just because we're doing this to make a baby doesn't mean it can't be fun, too."

This is Ryder. He's your friend. You can do this.

"I'm not sure about that," she said before she could stop herself. She wasn't certain if she was responding to his statement or answering herself.

"Don't worry," he said with a confident smile. "I'll make sure our lovemaking is enjoyable for both of us."

When Ryder lowered his head to lightly graze her lips with his, a jolt of awareness stronger than anything she had ever experienced instantly coursed through her. She told herself to take a step back, but when his mouth settled over hers to taste and tease, a delicious warmth began to pool in the pit of her stomach.

Lost in all the wonderful sensations swirling through her and unable to comprehend why she was experiencing them, it took a moment for her to realize that he had moved his hand to cover her breast. "Wh-what are you doing?" she asked, breaking the kiss.

"It's called foreplay, Summer." He kissed his way along her jaw to the side of her neck, then whispered in her ear, "Everything will be a lot easier and there's a better chance of success if we're both relaxed and ready to make love."

His warm breath feathering over her ear sent another wave of tingling heat crashing through her and caused her knees to wobble. "I hadn't thought it would be necessary," she said, wondering how she could feel excitement and apprehension at the same time.

Leaning back to look down at her, his dark green eyes held hers. "Are you a virgin, Summer?"

It was the last thing she expected him to ask. "No. Why?"

"Because I've never seen you this nervous," he said, pulling her to his wide chest. "How long has it been since you've been with a man?"

"I don't think that's relevant," she said, curious why her sexual experience, or lack thereof, mattered. "But if you have to know, I've only had sex a few times and that was my freshman year in college."

He nodded. "That explains why you're so tense. I'm betting the poor kid didn't have a clue what he was doing any more than you did. It wasn't all that good for you, was it?"

"No."

She decided to go along with his assumption. It was easier than admitting that her stress stemmed from the reprehensible act by one of the worst examples of his gender.

"I promise that it will be different for you this time," he said, bringing his hand up to thread his fingers through her hair. "I give you my word that I'll ensure your pleasure before I find my own."

Her heart beat double time. "D-don't worry about me. It's not necessary for me to—"

He shook his head as he started to tug the tail of her T-shirt from the waistband of her jeans. "I'm not a selfish man, Summer. Part of my satisfaction will be knowing that I've helped you find yours."

She closed her eyes. *You can do this. Just focus on your goal and you can do this.*

But when Ryder moved to lift the hem of her shirt to take it off her, she felt the hard evidence straining at his jeans and her nerves got the better of her. "I—I…can't," she said, beginning to tremble as she pushed away from him. "I can't do this. I thought I could…because I really want a baby. But I was wrong. I'm sorry. I just can't."

"Whoa! Slow down, darlin'," he said, releasing her shirt to place his hands on her shoulders. He stared at her for several long seconds. "Calm down and tell me what's wrong."

She tried to blink back a wave of tears as she stared into his concerned eyes. "I…just can't. I…want to. But I…can't."

Leading her over to the bed, he sat down and pulled her onto his lap. Cradling her to him as if she were a child, he held her close. "Talk to me, Summer. Tell me what's going on."

"I want a baby…but I just can't…do this, Ryder," she sobbed against his shoulder.

"It's okay, darlin'," he said, his tone gentle. "I give you my word nothing is going to happen that you don't want happening. Now, tell me what caused you to be so afraid."

"I was… I mean, I told him no," she stammered. "But he wouldn't stop."

She felt Ryder's body go completely still a moment

before he spoke in a voice so deadly quiet that it caused a cold chill to travel the length of her. "You were raped."

Unable to answer, she nodded.

"Was it your first experience?" he asked in the same cold tone.

"N-no. It was someone else." She took a shuddering breath. "I told him no, but we…were on a date. I'm not sure—"

"It doesn't matter if you were on a date or not," Ryder ground out, shaking his head. "No means no. If a man ignores that, then it's rape." His arms tightened around her. "When did it happen, darlin'?"

She hadn't talked about it with anyone. Not when the incident happened and not since. But apparently having suppressed it for so long, once she started talking about it, she couldn't seem to stop herself.

"It was at the end of my sophomore year in college. We were in a communication class together and he seemed nice enough. When he asked me out, I accepted." She shivered uncontrollably. "He turned out to be the worst mistake I've ever made."

"That's why you don't date and why you aren't interested in getting married, isn't it?" he asked, continuing to hold her protectively against him. "You're afraid of being intimate with a man."

"I've tried to get past my issues, but I'm not comfortable being alone with men," she said, swallowing hard. "I don't trust them."

"I'm a man and you've never had a problem being alone with me," he said, gently running his hand up and down her arm in a soothing manner.

"You're different," she said without hesitation.

He leaned back to look at her and she could tell his mock frown was meant to lighten the mood and make her feel a little better. "What do you think I am, darlin', a sexless old gelding?"

"No." For the first time since she'd agreed to his requirements, she smiled. "But you're my friend. I trust you."

His expression became serious. "And I promise that I'll never betray that trust, Summer."

Staring at each other for several long seconds, she finally said, "I still want a baby."

He nodded. "I figured you would."

"Where do we go from here? Will you still help me?" she asked, praying that he would.

"We'll talk more about this in the morning," he said evasively. "I just remembered that I promised my foreman the night off and I forgot to feed the horses."

"Do you need help?" she asked, disheartened that he had avoided answering her question.

"No." After setting her on her feet, he rose from the side of the bed, took her hand in his and led her out of the master suite. Then he walked her down to the room she had been using. "Sleep well, darlin'," he said, brushing her lips with his. "I'll see you in the morning."

Anger stronger than he had experienced in almost twenty years coursed through Ryder as he descended the stairs, grabbed a couple of cold beers from the refrigerator as he passed through the kitchen and stormed out of the house. He had done his best not to let Summer see the effect her telling him about the sexual assault had on him. For one thing, he didn't want to frighten her. And for another, the degree of fury that he felt toward the unnamed man had scared the living daylights out of him.

Entering the barn, he sat down on a bale of straw by the tack room and, popping the top on one of the cans, downed the contents. He knew the incident had taken place a couple of years before he and Summer had even met, but that didn't keep him from wanting to find the sorry son of a bitch and teach him a lesson he would never forget.

Ryder shook his head as he crushed the empty can, then tossing it aside, pulled the tab on the second can to take another swig of cold beer. Real men never took what a woman wasn't ready and willing to give. Period. When a woman told a man no, then he headed for a shower cold enough to cause frostbite, jogged until his shoes fell apart or bench-pressed a bulldozer if he had to in order to work off the adrenaline. And as far as Ryder was concerned, there were no excuses for doing anything else.

Feeling a little more in control, he leaned back against the barn wall. He hadn't liked lying to Summer about needing to feed the horses, but it couldn't be helped. He had needed the time and space to calm down and regain his equilibrium.

He couldn't help but remember another time when he had been filled with the same degree of anger and the consequences that he'd had to suffer through because of it. He had just turned fourteen and had been sent to live with a foster couple in Fort Worth. His foster mother had been real nice, but his foster dad had been a real piece of work. A functioning alcoholic, Pete Ledbetter held a job and to the outward eye everything was fine. But it hadn't taken Ryder long to realize that things weren't always as they seemed.

Pete usually stayed stone-cold sober during the day, but as soon as he got off work he started drinking and didn't stop until he passed out. Then he would sleep it off overnight, get up the next morning and the cycle would start all over again. But there were times before he passed out that Pete would turn into a mean drunk and made life a living hell around the Ledbetter home. Usually his wrath was directed at his wife and he left Ryder alone. Probably because even at the age of fourteen, Ryder was taller and more muscular than he was.

But the cycle was broken for good one fateful evening when Ryder came home after football practice and found Ellen Ledbetter sitting at the kitchen table nursing a black eye and a busted lip. She had told him that Pete was in a particularly nasty mood and that Ryder should make himself scarce until his foster father drank himself into oblivion.

Maybe his life would have turned out differently if he had listened to Ellen. But even at that young age, he had felt the need to protect those who were unable to defend themselves and when Pete walked in to take another swing at his wife, Ryder had stepped between them. The next thing he knew, Pete Ledbetter lay dead in a pool of blood on the kitchen floor, and Ryder was being handcuffed and hauled off to a juvenile detention center.

He took a deep breath and finished his beer. He had eventually been cleared of the involuntary manslaughter charge and sent to the Last Chance Ranch, but the incident had changed his life forever. From that moment forward, he had never raised his fists in anger at any time, for any reason.

He'd had no trouble keeping that promise to himself. Hell, he hadn't even been tempted to go back on it. At least, not until Summer told him about the man who raped her. Ryder knew beyond a shadow of doubt that if he could have gotten hold of the bastard, he would have torn him apart with his bare hands. And that bothered him.

But what scared him more was Summer finding out that he wasn't the person she thought him to be. How would she react if she discovered that the man she trusted above all others had caused another man's death?

Just the thought of watching the revulsion cloud her pretty blue eyes caused a knot the size of his fist to twist his gut. That's why he never intended for her to know about the incident. He couldn't stand the thought of losing her. And he had no doubt that's exactly what would happen if she learned the truth about him.

Five

When Summer finished helping Betty Lou make sandwiches for a picnic lunch, she walked down the hall to Ryder's study. He had been busy making a list of things he wanted his foreman to take care of over the next week while he was working the rodeo with her up in Oklahoma. They hadn't had the opportunity to discuss what had happened last night, but after telling him about the assault she'd done a lot of thinking and had a few things she wanted to talk over with him before they left the Blue Canyon Ranch.

The study door was open and, knocking on the door frame, she stepped into the room. "Ryder, I just finished helping Betty Lou make lunch for us. Do you have time to ride down to the canyon for another picnic?"

When he looked up and smiled, she caught her

breath. He was without a doubt one of the best-looking men she'd ever seen.

"That sounds like a great idea," he said, rising to his feet. He picked up a paper from the desk and walked over to her. "I need to drop this repair list off with my foreman anyway and while I'm down at the barn I'll saddle the horses." His expression turned serious. "I didn't want to ask this morning in front of Betty Lou, but are you feeling better?"

His concern touched her. "I'm fine," she said. "It seems that finally telling someone about what happened was a bit cathartic for me."

He frowned. "You hadn't told anyone? Why didn't you report the assault to the authorities?"

"Besides just wanting to forget that night ever happened, I wasn't sure they would believe me since I was on a date with him," she said, shaking her head.

Wrapping his strong arms around her, Ryder pulled her to his wide chest for a comforting hug. "That's a lot to have to carry by yourself for all these years. You should have told someone, darlin'."

"I guess I was…ashamed that I had been so naive," she said, hugging him back.

When he released her, he shook his head. "You didn't do anything to be ashamed of, Summer. It wasn't your fault and I don't want you thinking that is was."

Shrugging, she fell into step with him as they walked down the hall to the kitchen. "I suppose you're right."

"I know I am," he said vehemently. "Now, while I'm getting the horses ready, you pack the saddlebags and I'll meet you down at the barn."

An hour later as they dismounted the horses beside the lazy little creek on the canyon floor, Summer felt as if she had turned a corner in her life. She only hoped that Ryder would support her decision and still agree to help her.

"This seemed like a nice place the last time," he said, spreading the blanket in the same spot they had picnicked a couple of days before.

"I love that the trees are just beginning to change colors," she murmured, looking around at a few golden leaves on the cottonwood trees. "I think autumn is the prettiest time of year."

"We'll have to come back in a couple of weeks," he said as he lowered himself onto the blanket. "Just about every tree in this canyon will be a bright gold."

"I'll look forward to it." She couldn't help but feel heartened by the fact that he was making plans for them to come back together in the future. "I'm sure it will be beautiful."

While they ate, they exchanged small talk about the upcoming rodeo they would both be working and some of the plans Ryder had for the ranch. Summer enjoyed hearing about the projects he wanted to undertake, but couldn't seem to get her mind off what she needed to discuss with him.

Deciding that there was no easy way to start the conversation, she took a deep breath. "Last night after you left the house to feed the horses, I did a lot of soul-searching," she admitted as she gathered the remnants of their lunch. "And I still want a baby."

He planted his feet at the edge of the blanket and

rested his arms on his bent knees. "That's what you said last night."

"Are you still willing to father my child?" she asked, mentally holding her breath as she awaited his answer.

"I gave you my word and that hasn't changed," he said. "But I won't hold you to our having to make love for you to become pregnant. If you'll make the appointment with your doctor, I'll go get cozy with a specimen cup." She could tell it wasn't in the least bit appealing to him, but he was willing to do it in order to keep her from feeling uncomfortable, as well as honor his commitment to her.

She nibbled on her lower lip a moment before finding the nerve to tell him what she had decided the night before. "Actually, that isn't what I want you to do."

One dark eyebrow rose in question as he slowly turned his head to stare at her. "What are you saying?"

"I'm tired of being afraid, Ryder," she said, knowing it was true. "I'm not sure how this is going to sound, but I want to be a whole woman again. If you're willing, I'd like for you to help me get over my fear of intimacy." She could tell from the look on his face that he was thoroughly shocked by her proclamation. "I think that can be accomplished if we have sex in order to conceive."

"Darlin', I can understand you wanting to go through with having a baby," he said quietly. "And I get that you don't want to be afraid anymore. But are you really sure about this?"

"Yes."

He remained silent for several long moments before he spoke again. "You do realize that it's probably going to take more than one lovemaking session for you to become pregnant?"

She nodded. "I'm aware of that, but I started thinking about something you said when you first agreed to help me…and I realize artificial insemination isn't what I want."

"I say a lot of things, but that doesn't mean I'm always right," he admitted.

"But in this case, you were," she insisted. "You told me that you would like to be able to tell our child that we purposely came together because we wanted him or her, not because a doctor intervened with a clinical procedure." She smiled. "I think it will mean more to our child when he or she is old enough to understand."

He hesitated for a moment before he asked, "Do you still want to get started right away?"

She didn't have to think about her answer. "Yes."

"Then I think instead of you staying in a hotel room, from now on you should stay with me in my camper," he said, meeting her startled gaze. Ryder was one of the many cowboys and rodeo personnel who preferred to travel with their own accommodations, rather than rent a hotel room.

"There's only one drawback to that," she countered. "Everyone will think that we've taken our friendship to the next level."

It took her by surprise when he laughed out loud. "What the hell do you think they'll say when they find out we're having a baby together?"

"I really hadn't thought much about that," she admitted.

"You know how close rodeo people are," he said pointedly. "Word will get around. It's not something we can hide, nor do I intend to try. When your pregnancy starts to show, I'm going to proudly tell people that I'm the daddy, not make it seem like it's an accident from our sneaking around."

What he said made sense. But she had avoided rumors of anything going on between them for so long that old habits were hard to break.

"All right," she said, realizing he was probably right. She didn't want people to think their child was the mistake of a clandestine affair, either. "I guess that settles everything."

Ryder surprised her when he shook his head. "Nope. There's one more thing that we haven't covered."

"What would that be?" For the life of her, she couldn't imagine what there was left to be decided after their countless conversations on the subject.

"We're going to start acting like we're a couple," he stated.

"You mean as if we've fallen in love?" Things just kept getting more and more complicated by the moment.

"It's easier to go with that, than it is to try and explain everything." He leaned over and briefly pressed his lips to hers. "Besides, that's what people are going to think anyway. We might as well go along with it."

"Does that mean we'll be openly affectionate toward each other?" she asked, liking the way his kiss made her tingle all over.

"Yup. That's what people do when they're…involved."

She furrowed her brow. "Do you think we can be convincing?"

"Let's see," he said, lowering his head.

He kissed her again, but this time it wasn't a chaste brushing of the lips between two friends. This time it was the kiss of a man asking a woman to trust him, asking her to let him show her that intimacy didn't have to be feared.

Closing her eyes, Summer forced herself to relax and experience his gentle caress. She knew without question that if she asked him to stop, he would do so in a heartbeat. But that wasn't what she wanted. She wasn't entirely certain why, but for the first time in years, she needed to feel like a real woman again, instead of the frightened female she had become after the assault.

Ryder teased her with his tongue until she parted her lips on a sigh, then slipping inside, he gently explored her tender inner recesses. She didn't even try to stop herself from melting against him. She had avoided men for so long that she had forgotten how nice it was to feel safe in a man's arms, to feel cherished.

"I don't think we'll have any problems convincing anyone that we've taken our friendship to the next level," he said, easing away from the kiss.

"There isn't anyone around right now for us to impress," she said breathlessly. "Why—"

"I thought we could use the practice." His wide grin sent a wave of goose bumps shimmering over her skin. "Besides, I decided you needed to be reminded that kissing is just plain fun."

He rose to his feet, then held his hand out to help her

to hers. Summer didn't even think to hesitate before she placed her hand, as well as her complete trust, in his. They had crossed a line in their friendship, and there was no going back now. The only thing left to do was move forward and see where this latest twist in their relationship took them.

When he and Summer rode the horses back into the ranch yard, Ryder groaned inwardly at the sight of his brother's truck parked beside his own. What was Lane doing here?

"It looks like one of my brother's is going to be the first one to learn about the new development in our friendship," he said as they dismounted and led the horses into the barn.

"Do you think he'll be convinced?" she asked, unsaddling the buckskin mare.

Ryder laughed, releasing some of the tension building across his shoulders. "The other night at Sam and Bria's party, I couldn't convince any of my brothers otherwise. So, no. I don't think we'll have a problem getting him to believe there's something more going on between us." As an afterthought, he added, "But it wouldn't hurt to test-drive our show of affection toward each other."

"In other words, you don't want me freaking out when you put your arm around me?" she asked.

"Or when I kiss you in front of him," he said, nodding.

Summer looked thoughtful for a moment. "That's

why you were irritated with your brothers at the party, wasn't it? They were speculating on our relationship."

"Yup." He led the horses back into their stalls, then draping his arm across her shoulders, started walking them toward the house. "And you can bet by supper tonight, Lane will have reported back to every one of them and let them know that their speculations were right on the money."

She grinned. "Wouldn't you do the same if you discovered something about one of them?"

He laughed as they climbed the steps to the back porch. "Darlin', I wouldn't be able to dial the phone fast enough."

When they entered the kitchen, Lane was seated at the table having a cup of coffee with Betty Lou. "Hey you two, I was beginning to think I was going to miss seeing you," he said, rising to his feet. Nodding at Summer, he added, "It's nice seeing you again, Ms. Patterson."

"Please, call me Summer. And it's nice seeing you again, too, Lane." She smiled at Ryder. "While you visit with your brother, I think I'm going upstairs to take advantage of the Jacuzzi before I help Betty Lou with dinner."

Ryder pulled her to him and covered her mouth with his. He told himself the kiss was for his brother's benefit, but as Summer's lips clung to his, he knew that was a bald-faced lie. The kiss they had shared under the cottonwood tree had left him aching to kiss her again and he couldn't resist seizing the opportunity now.

"I'll see you in a little while, darlin'," he said against her soft lips.

As Summer left the room, he turned back to Lane and almost laughed out loud. For a professional poker player who prided himself on his ability not to show any emotion, Lane was failing miserably. He looked like he had just been treated to the business end of an electric cattle prod. For that matter, so did Betty Lou.

"What?" Ryder asked, feigning ignorance.

The first to recover, his housekeeper got up from the table and walking up to him, patted his cheek. "I'm glad to see you finally woke up," she said, grinning from ear to ear. "You and that little girl are gonna make a real fine couple. The way you always talked about her whenever you came home from a rodeo, I knew it was just a matter of time before you realized there was more going on between the two of you than just being good friends."

When Betty Lou walked on past him to enter the pantry, Ryder turned to see his brother grinning at him like a damned fool. "What's up, bro?" he asked, already knowing he was about to face an inquisition.

"Why don't we grab a couple of beers and go into your office for that visit?" Lane asked, pointing toward the hall. "You can tell me once again that you and Summer are just good friends and I can tell you that you're full of bullroar and buffalo chips."

"I can already tell you're going to be a jerk about this, aren't you?" Ryder groused as he got them both a cold beer and they headed toward his office.

"Oh yeah. But you wouldn't expect anything less from me," Lane shot back. He lowered his lanky frame into the armchair in front of Ryder's desk. "If you had the chance, you'd do the same thing to me or any of the other guys."

Grinning, Ryder nodded. "You bet your sweet ass I would."

Lane took a swallow from his beer bottle. "So what's the story with you and Summer?" He gave Ryder a knowing look. "Since Betty Lou was just as surprised as I was, I take it that you two just started dating?"

Ryder propped his booted feet on the edge of the desk, then crossing his legs at the ankles, leaned back in his desk chair. "We just started thinking of each other as more than friends in the past couple of days." Frowning, he added, "Apparently you guys saw something that night at the party that I didn't because we didn't start talking about taking things up a notch until we were on the way back here."

His brother nodded. "I watched her watching you and I could tell friendship was the last thing on her mind."

"Okay," Ryder said, holding up both hands in surrender. He wasn't about to tell Lane that she'd had something on her mind all right. She had been sizing him up as a prize stud, instead of the romantic encounter his brothers all thought. "I was wrong and you all were right. Does that make you happy?"

"You have no idea how much," Lane answered glibly. "The next time Bria has a family dinner for all of us, you can expect to be the one in the hot seat."

"When you leave here, you won't even make it to the main road before you tell the rest of the guys about this, will you?" Ryder asked, knowing it was already as good as a done deal.

Lane laughed out loud as he shook his head. "You know good and well that finding out something like this has got to be shared. And the sooner, the better."

Ryder knew that if he asked Lane not to tell their brothers, he would keep the confidence. Being a licensed psychologist, Lane knew how to listen and keep his mouth shut. But as much as he dreaded the ribbing he would take from his brothers, Ryder realized it was the best way to get the word out that he and Summer had taken their friendship to the next level and would set the stage for her becoming pregnant.

"Enough about me, what are you up to?" Ryder asked, realizing it was time to change the subject.

"After you two left the party the other night, Bria decided that we all needed to take some cake home with us and I volunteered to bring yours by on my way to Shreveport," Lane replied, checking his gold Rolex. "And that reminds me, I need to get on the road so I can get to the casino and get checked in."

"Are you playing in another big tournament this week?" Ryder asked.

"Not this time." Frowning, Lane set his half-empty beer bottle on the desk. "It's the damnedest thing. Last week, I got a written invitation to a private game with Ben Cunningham."

Ryder recognized the name of one of the most famous players in the world of professional poker. "I thought Cunningham retired."

"So did I." Lane rose to his feet. "But I'm not going

to turn down the chance to play a game with arguably the best player in the history of poker."

"I don't blame you," Ryder said, following his brother down the hall to the kitchen. "It's not every day you're invited to play with a legend. Good luck."

"Thanks, but you know I don't rely on Lady Luck. She's too fickle. I'd much rather use my skills. At least that way I have a fighting chance of winning." Turning to Betty Lou standing at the counter cutting up vegetables, Lane touched the wide brim of his black Resistol. "Betty Lou, you take care and if you have any problems with this big lug, just give me a call. I'll line him out in short order."

"You and whose army?" Ryder laughed, following Lane out to the porch.

"You're working a rodeo at one of the county fairs up in Oklahoma this weekend, aren't you?" Lane asked, his easy expression turning serious.

Ryder nodded. "Why?"

"Nate and Jaron are planning on competing in the bull and bareback riding events. You might want to keep an eye on Nate," he said, starting down the steps. "He's not quite up to par these days."

"What's up with him?" Of all his brothers, Nate was the last one to take life too seriously and Ryder couldn't imagine anything bringing him down for very long.

"That little nurse he's been seeing down in Waco broke things off with him the day after the party and he's not taking it very well," Lane explained.

"Wounded pride?" Ryder asked, a little surprised by the news. To his knowledge, it was the first time that

Nate had been dumped. Normally, he was the one initiating a breakup when things looked like they might be getting too serious.

"I'm not so sure," Lane answered. "There was something about the way Nate looked when he talked about her that led me to believe he had started feeling more for her than he had any other woman."

"I'll be sure to keep an extra close eye on him," Ryder promised as Lane walked to his truck.

Watching his brother's truck disappear down the driveway as Lane headed toward the main road, Ryder felt his protective instincts come to full alert and made a mental vow to be extra vigilant during the bull riding event. Being around the rough stock while nursing a broken heart wasn't a good mix. They had all learned that firsthand a few months back when Sam had been run down by one of the meanest bulls his rodeo stock contracting company had to offer. The accident had ultimately led to his brother and Bria working out their marital problems, but Ryder would just as soon not see another one of his brothers sustain a life-threatening injury as a result of a romantic breakup.

"I'm getting too old for this," he muttered as he turned to go back inside the house.

But as long as he had breath in his body, he knew he would do whatever it took to keep his family safe from harm. And that included Summer and their as-yet-to-be-conceived child.

Summer had just finished packing her luggage for the trip with Ryder when the sound of him bellowing like an outraged bull came from somewhere downstairs. As she rushed out into the hall the sound of glass breaking, accompanied by his guttural curse, sent her running to see what had happened. Her heart thumped inside her chest as fear began to course through her veins. What on earth could have happened? Was he hurt?

"Will somebody get this damned cat off me?" Ryder shouted when she found him at the bottom of the staircase.

He was twisting around like a whirling dervish as he tried to reach behind him where Lucifer clung to the middle of his back. The cat screeched and hissed almost as loudly as the rapid-fire curse words Ryder continued to spew out.

"Hold still," Betty Lou commanded, hurrying in from the kitchen. Stepping around the shards of a shattered vase that Ryder and Lucifer had knocked off a console table, she carefully tried to disentangle the cat's claws from the fabric of Ryder's shirt. When she finally lifted the cat from his back, she motioned for Summer to step in. "While I get Lucifer calmed down and clean up this glass, see what you can do about smoothing Ryder's ruffled feathers."

"Are you all right?" Summer asked. "Did you get cut by the glass when the vase broke?"

"No, I'm fine." He scowled. "I swear that cat hates me. And I'm beginning to return the feeling."

"Take off your shirt," she said, noticing some drops of blood dotting the back of it. "Your back is bleeding."

"I'm okay," he insisted, rotating his shoulders. "It's just a few scratches."

"I'm not going to argue with you, Ryder." Why did men have to be so darned stubborn about these things?

"Really, darlin', it's no big deal," he said.

Losing patience, she took him by the hand to lead him up the stairs. "Any time there's a break in the skin, it could become infected. We need to put antibiotic ointment on those scratches."

"I don't see what all the fuss is about," he complained as they entered the master suite and he turned on the bedside lamp. "But if you insist, there should be something in the medicine cabinet in the bathroom."

"Take off your shirt while I go get the ointment," she commanded.

When she found the tube and returned to the bedroom, she stopped short at the sight of Ryder with his shirt off, sitting on the end of the bed. In all of her twenty-five years, she didn't think she had ever seen a more beautiful specimen of a man in his prime. She'd felt the rock hard strength he had been hiding behind his chambray shirts when he held her, but nothing could have prepared her for the perfection of his well-defined chest and finely sculpted abdominal muscles.

She'd known he was in excellent physical condition. He had to be, considering the agility and athleticism required for his job as a bullfighter. But she had never given a thought to how all that would translate to his physique. With his broad shoulders, rippling abs and bulging biceps, he had a body most men envied and women wished their significant other had.

"Summer, are you all right?"

Embarrassed that he had caught her staring, she nodded. "I was wondering if I should go back for bandages."

"No." He shook his head as he turned for her to put the ointment on his back. "I really don't think I need the salve either, but if it makes you feel better, go ahead and put some on the scratches."

"I thought you said you always look up to see where Lucifer is before you walk past the stairs," she said to distract herself. The feel of his warm, firm skin beneath her fingertips caused a pleasant tingling in the pit of her belly and she could swear the temperature in the room had gone up by several degrees.

"Normally, I do make sure I know where he is." Ryder shrugged. "I guess I was distracted about getting things ready so we can take off early tomorrow morning."

"How early is early?" she asked, capping the tube of ointment.

"It's a good six hours' drive up to the fairgrounds where the rodeo is being held, so I'd say we better leave around four or five in the morning." Turning to face her, he smiled as he reached to pull her down onto his lap. "Don't you have to be there by noon?"

"I have to…set up interviews with the local newspaper and…radio stations." With all that bare masculine skin pressed against her side, she was having a little trouble catching her breath. "But that seems awfully… early to be leaving."

"You normally fly when you leave one town to go to

the next one on the rodeo schedule." He grinned. "Road trips take a little longer."

It had been so long since she had traveled by car between the many cities and towns on the circuit, she had forgotten they would need extra time. "I'll be sure to set my alarm," she said, starting to get up from his lap.

He tightened his arms around her to hold her in place. "Don't worry about it. I'll just roll over and wake you."

Her breath lodged in her lungs as she stared at him. She had thought they were going to wait until she stayed with him in his camper before they started trying for her to conceive. But as his green gaze held hers, she realized it was probably for the best that she hadn't had time to anticipate their first time together. There was a very real possibility that if she knew too far in advance her anxiety level would go sky-high and she would lose her nerve again.

Taking a deep breath, she nodded. "I'll go get my pajamas."

"I've been thinking about how to go about getting you past some of your fear," he said slowly. "And I think a compromise is in order."

She wasn't entirely certain she was going to like what he had to say next. But before she could ask what he had in mind, he told her.

"I mentioned that I like to sleep in the buff and you apparently like to be covered up from neck to ankles." He gave her a smile that curled her toes inside her cross trainers. "I'll wear underwear to bed and you can wear your panties and one of my undershirts."

Her heart fluttered wildly. “How is that going to accomplish getting me past the fear of having sex?”

“Before we go any further with this, let’s get one thing straight, darlin’.” He shook his head. “We aren’t going to be having sex. We’re going to make love.”

“It’s the same thing, isn’t it?” she asked, frowning.

He hugged her close. “Sex is nothing but mechanics.” His tone was so low and intimate it sent shivers of anticipation up her spine. “Making love is two people coming together to bring each other pleasure and to enjoy the shared experience.”

She doubted that would be the case for her, but she wasn’t going to argue with him. She was still trying to get past the idea of both of them sleeping in the same bed with so little on.

“You still haven’t answered my question,” she said, finally finding her voice. “How is sleeping in the same bed and wearing so little going to get me past my fear?”

Kissing the top of her head, his deep chuckle seemed to vibrate all the way to her soul. “What do people normally wear when they’re making love?”

“Nothing,” she said automatically.

He nodded. “And I’m betting that thought bothers you. A lot.”

“I…um…well, it does make me a little uncomfortable thinking about it,” she admitted.

“Don’t you think that us wearing at least a few things to bed would be easier for you in the beginning than if we wore nothing at all?” he asked.

Being naked together wasn’t something she had allowed herself to think about before and she wasn't sure she wanted to now. "You're probably right."

When he used his index finger to lift her chin until their eyes met, he asked huskily, "Do you still trust me, Summer?"

She didn't have to think twice about her answer. "Yes."

"Then let's try this." He smiled. "If it doesn't work, then we can always make that appointment with your doctor."

Setting her on her feet, he stood up and, walking over to the dresser, opened one of the drawers. "Here," he said, handing her one of his white cotton undershirts. "While you change and get into bed, I'll go downstairs and turn off the lights."

As she watched Ryder leave the room, she knew he was giving her the time to come to terms with his reasoning. And she had to admit his idea made sense. But as she went into the master bathroom to put the ointment back into the medicine cabinet and change into his undershirt, she wasn't overly confident that it would work.

Hurrying to take off her clothes and put on his shirt, she had just crawled into bed and pulled the comforter up to her chin when Ryder walked into the bedroom and closed the door. "Did Betty Lou get the pieces of the vase cleaned up?" she asked. "I should have helped her with that."

He nodded. "She had everything cleared away and was giving Lucifer a cat treat when I got down there." He shook his head as he sat on the side of the bed to take off his boots. "Can you believe it? He uses me as a scratching post and then gets some kind of reward for doing it."

She appreciated Ryder talking as if they were holding a conversation over coffee instead of getting ready to sleep together. It helped keep her mind off what was about to happen.

"Did you want Betty Lou to give you a cat treat?" she asked, unable to stop a nervous giggle.

Looking over his shoulder at her, he grimaced. "I'm glad to hear you're having a good laugh at my expense." He stood up to remove his jeans. "But you forgot one thing, darlin'."

"Wh-what's that?" she managed to get out as she watched him shove the denim down to his ankles.

"There's this thing called retribution," he said, kicking the garment aside, then turning to stretch out on the bed beside her. Grinning, he reached for her as he added, "And I happen to know just how to even the score."

Apprehension coursed through her a moment before Ryder moved his fingers over her ribs and she dissolved into a fit of laughter. "St-stop," she shrieked as she tried to get away. No match for his strength, she gasped for breath. "Why did I ever…tell you…I'm…ticklish?"

"I don't know, but I'm glad you did." His grin faded as his fingers stilled and his green eyes darkened to a forest-green. "I'm going to kiss you, Summer."

Her pulse sped up as he slowly lowered his head. But the moment their lips met, she eyes drifted shut and she lost herself in the kiss. Moving his mouth over hers, the tenderness and care that he took exploring her brought tears to her eyes. Every time he kissed her it was as if he reaffirmed his commitment to help her get over the assault that had held her prisoner for the past several years.

Using his tongue, he coaxed her to open for him and when she did, the touch of his tongue to hers sent tiny charges of electric current skipping over every nerve ending in her body. But instead of stroking her inner recesses as she expected, he engaged her in a game of advance and retreat as if daring her to do some exploring of her own. As she tentatively followed his lead, she felt his big body shudder when her tongue entered his mouth to taste and tease.

Lost in the heady feeling of being in charge, it took a moment for her to realize that his hand was moving along her side. When he paused at the underside of her breast before cupping its weight in his palm, she caught her breath. The cotton undershirt he had given her to put on was the only barrier between her hardened nipple and his calloused hand, but instead of causing the panicked feeling she expected, a delicious heat began to pool in the pit of her stomach.

The delightful sensations might have continued had she not moved her leg and come into contact with the hard evidence of his arousal straining at his boxer briefs. Her heart skipped a beat and breaking the kiss, she waited to see what happened next.

To her surprise, instead of taking things further, Ryder continued to chafe the tip of her breast as he gave her a brief kiss. Then, removing his hand, he whispered close to her ear, "Don't worry, darlin'. I'm in complete control."

"Are you… I mean, are we going to—"

He held her close as he rolled to his back. "Not tonight."

She couldn't understand the sudden tangle of emotions coursing through her. On one hand, she was relieved that they weren't going to make love. And on the other, she was slightly disappointed. It was the disappointment that she found so confusing.

"Why not?" she asked before she could stop herself.

"Because you're not ready," he said, reaching over to turn off the bedside lamp.

"But you are."

"It doesn't matter." His low chuckle as he pulled the comforter over them caused warmth to spread throughout her chest. "We won't be making love until we're both ready." He pressed a kiss to the top of her head, pillowed on his shoulder. "Now, I suggest you get some sleep because morning will be here before you know it."

Long after she heard Ryder's soft snores, Summer lay awake thinking about his plan to help her overcome her fears. He wasn't going to rush her. He was giving her the time she needed to get used to the idea of sleeping in the same bed with him, used to having him hold and touch her. She knew it had to cost him some measure of physical discomfort, but he was willing to suffer through whatever it took to help her. An unfamiliar emotion began to spread throughout her chest at the thought. How many men would take that kind of care with a woman? Be that understanding?

Feeling more safe and secure than she had in years, she snuggled closer to him. He was her best friend and if she hadn't known that before, she certainly did after his honorable gesture.

But as she started to drift off into a peaceful sleep, her last thought was that she and Ryder had passed a turning point in their relationship—one that neither of them had seen coming and there was no way of reversing now.

Six

"Nate, you look like you don't know whether you lost a horse or just found a halter," Ryder said, spotting his brother leaning against the outside of the arena fence. Normally the most carefree of his brothers, Nate didn't appear to have his head in the game and that could spell disaster for a bull rider. "What's up?"

"Nothing," Nate answered, looking up. He replaced his serious expression with a smile. "I've just been mentally reviewing what I know about the bull I drew for today's round. That's all."

To the outward eye, most anyone would think Nate was shooting straight with them. Ryder knew better. There was a shadow in his brother's eyes that he had never seen before, and Nate's easy expression looked forced.

Lane had been right. There was more going on with

Nate than a case of wounded pride over being dumped for the first time in his life.

Ryder claimed a space along the fence next to his brother and, leaning back against it, folded his arms across his chest. "You want to talk about it?"

"Nope." To his brother's credit, Nate didn't try to deny there was more going on with him than thinking about the bull he'd drawn.

He hadn't expected his brother to open up to him and it wasn't Ryder's style to push the issue. "You know I'll have your back out there. But just in case, keep your mind on business or turn out and call it a day. There's no sense in either one of us getting hurt if you're not up for this."

His suggestion that Nate have the bull released into the arena without riding him when it came his turn, produced the result Ryder had been looking for. Determination had replaced the shadow in Nate's gaze.

"Like hell I will," Nate retorted, shoving away from the fence. "I've never turned out and I'm not about to start now." Squaring his shoulders, he gave Ryder his familiar cocky grin. "You better take your own advice and be a little more careful, brother. You're the one with the sexy lady waiting on you when the round is over."

"Talked to Lane, did you?" Ryder asked. He had expected Nate to mention the new development between himself and Summer at some point.

Nodding, Nate reached behind his thigh to buckle his leather chaps, then did the same with the other leg. "Yeah, Lane was in charge of holding the money for the pool."

"So what was the bet and which one of you won?"

Ryder wasn't the least bit surprised that his brothers had been making wagers on his relationship with Summer. They all made bets with each other on just about everything. Always had and probably always would.

"The bet was a hundred bucks each on how long it would take for you to wake up," Nate answered, laughing. "Jaron won."

"What did I win?" Jaron asked, walking over to join them.

"The pool where you all bet on when I'd wake up and realize Summer is more than my best friend," Ryder said, shaking his head. "So what's the next bet?"

"When the two of you tie the knot," Nate and Jaron both said in unison.

"I've got Thanksgiving," Jaron said, grinning.

Nate nodded. "If you could just hold out until Christmas, I'd appreciate it. I could use the money for Christmas presents."

"I hope you aren't holding your breath for either one of those dates," Ryder grumbled as he turned toward his camper to change into his bullfighting gear. "You'll both turn blue and pass out before that happens."

As he walked the distance to the designated camping area where he'd parked his trailer, he hoped that his talk with Nate helped his brother regain his focus. Otherwise, Nate would end up in a heap on the ground about two jumps into his eight-second ride, and Ryder would be responsible for saving his tail end from being run down by a ton of ornery beef.

Quickly changing into his protective undergear and

the uniform supplied by one of the rodeo association's sponsors, Ryder tied his running cleats, then grabbing his black Resistol, headed back to the arena. That's when he spotted Summer with her electronic tablet, directing photographers where they could safely stand for their action shots.

Watching her, he would be the first to admit she was pretty damned awesome. Every rodeo she coordinated ran like a well-oiled machine and there wasn't a doubt in anyone's mind who was in charge. She was the epitome of self-confidence and had no trouble ordering around men twice her size. That's why it had come as a shock to learn that her strength and self-assuredness didn't extend to her personal life, as well.

He couldn't help but wince when he thought about his role in helping her regain her courage in that particular area. For the past few nights, he had lain awake with his arms around her and his body urging him to sink himself into her softness. But he had promised they would both be ready before they took things to the next level. And he wasn't about to betray that trust, no matter how much his body ached.

Fortunately, he didn't think it would be much longer before she was comfortable enough with him to make love. If her snuggling against him at night was any indication, she trusted him without hesitation. And as far as he was concerned, a woman placing her complete trust in a man was what made the difference between making love and just having sex.

"Hey, cowboy," she said when she looked up to find him watching her. "Are you ready to dance?"

He nodded. "Yup. Dances With Bulls at your service, ma'am."

She reached up to brush a piece of lint from his black shirt. "I'm glad the rodeo association opted to have bullfighters wear these jerseys and athletic shorts. The job you do is too important for you to dress like a clown."

"Yeah, I guess it's hard to take a guy's job all that serious when he's wearing more makeup than most women," he said, grinning.

"Well, now that you mention it, that is a factor," she chuckled. Then her expression turned serious. "Please be careful, Ryder."

When the announcement came across the PA system that bull riding would be the next event, he leaned down and pressed his lips to hers. "Don't worry, darlin'. I understand those old bulls better than I do most people."

Turning, he jogged into the arena and, taking his position beside the chute gates, focused on the task at hand. He could give more thought to Summer's uncharacteristic plea for him to be careful after he'd done his job. Right now, he had over two dozen cowboys, including two of his brothers, counting on him to protect them from animals that had nothing more on their minds than making roadkill out of the person who had the audacity to try to ride them.

"Good luck," he called when he noticed Jaron was in the first group of riders.

"Thanks," his brother answered with a wave of his hand. "I'm going to need it with this one."

With his adrenaline level at its peak, Ryder stepped in when Jaron successfully rode his bull for the full eight seconds. Deftly dodging the animal's sharp horns, he ensured that his brother had time to sprint to the fence and out of danger before he lured the bull to the open gate leading out of the arena.

"Thanks, bro," Jaron said, jumping from his perch on the fence to gather his bull rope and wait for his score to be posted.

"All in a day's work," Ryder replied, grinning as he exchanged a high five with his brother.

As the afternoon wore on, he and the other bull-fighter working the event managed to distract one angry bull after another and keep the riders protected from getting stomped or gored. With only one bull rider left to ride in the day round, Ryder watched Nate climb on the back of Freight Train, a big, black bull known for running over whoever had the misfortune to get in his way.

He hoped Nate's mind was on taking care of business, but when his brother nodded that he was ready and the gate swung open, Ryder knew immediately that Nate was in serious trouble. His balance was off and when the bull went into a flat spin, Ryder's gut clenched as he watched Nate slide down into the well. Being on the inside of the spin was one of the most dangerous places a bull rider could find himself, and to make matters worse, Nate's hand was hung up in the bull rope.

Without a thought to his own safety, Ryder jumped into action, and while the other bullfighter tried to divert the angry animal out of the spin, he ran alongside the bull and worked on the rope to dislodge Nate's hand. Thankfully, Nate had managed to regain his footing when the bull stopped spinning and switched directions to chase the other bullfighter. But when Ryder finally managed to free his brother from the rope, Nate dropped to his knees, making him completely helpless if the bull decided to turn his attention back to the man who had tried to ride him.

"Get up and haul ass, Nate!" Ryder shouted as the bull turned toward him.

Slapping the bull's nose to keep its attention on him, Ryder continued to taunt the animal until he was certain Nate had made it to safety. Only then did he and the other bullfighter maneuver the bull toward the open gate leading out of the arena and back to the holding pens.

Angry with Nate for even attempting the ride when his mind was elsewhere, Ryder was glad that the events were over for the day. Jogging out of the arena, he had every intention of finding his brother and giving him a good tongue-lashing for putting them both in more danger than was necessary.

"Thank goodness you made it out of there without getting injured!" Summer cried, running up to him.

Ryder stopped when he noticed that she was trembling. His problem with Nate's carelessness forgotten, he took her into his arms and hugged her close.

"I'm fine, darlin'." Leaning back to look down at her, he brushed a lock of her honey-blond hair from her creamy cheek. "You've seen me in a lot worse situations than that one. What was there about this time that scared you?"

"I'm not sure, but..." Frowning, she paused for a moment like she might be as surprised by her reaction as he was. "...it seemed to take forever for you to free Nate and for all of you to make it to safety."

"But we made it just fine," Ryder assured her. He looked around as he searched for his brother. "Although, when I get the chance, I've got some choice things to say to Nate that he's not going to be all that fine with."

"I think he and Jaron are already on their way to the training room to gather their things," she said. "Will he be competing tomorrow?"

Ryder nodded. "I'll catch him then." He gave her a kiss, then stepped back. "Right now, I'd better go get a quick shower and change before the barbecue and dance."

"I'll be waiting." Her sweet smile and the promise in her cornflower-blue eyes caused heat to coil low in his belly.

As he turned toward the camping area, one thought kept running through his mind. He was in real trouble if all it took to rev up his libido was one little smile. He had another endless evening ahead of him, holding and kissing her without being able to make love to her.

Ryder shook his head as he entered the camper and went straight to the small shower to turn on the cold water. "It's going to be a long night," he muttered as he stripped out of his uniform and stepped under the stinging spray. He sucked in a sharp breath. "One hell of a long night."

One of the many things Summer liked about her job was the fact that nearly every rodeo had a barbecue and dance after the Saturday events. It didn't matter what town they were in, tables were always piled high with all kinds of food, the scent of burning mesquite hung on the crisp night air, and the live band, although not always the best, played with enough enthusiasm no one cared. Tonight was no different, except for one little detail. Tonight she wasn't with Ryder as just his friend. They were acting like a couple.

Amazingly, no one had appeared to be all that surprised by the change in their relationship status. Not even when they arrived together hand in hand or when they chose a table off to themselves.

After dining on some of the most delicious food she could ever remember, she and Ryder watched the band tune their guitars and adjust their microphones in preparation for the dance to begin. When she glanced up, he was smiling at her.

"Do you have any idea how pretty you are?" he asked, covering her hand with his where it rested on the table.

Her heart skipped a beat at his compliment and the feel of his warm, calloused palm against her much smoother skin. It caused a pleasant tingling to spread throughout her body. "Thank you." She smiled. "You clean up real nice yourself, cowboy."

Her breath caught when she realized they were actually flirting with each other. Was this part of Ryder's plan? Were they role-playing for the benefit of one of their coworkers?

Looking around, she didn't think so. There wasn't anyone they knew close enough to overhear their conversation. Frowning, she realized that for her, their flirting had felt very real.

Before she could speculate further on the matter, he stood up when the band started playing a slow number and held out his hand. "Can I have this dance, darlin'?"

As she stared up at him, her pulse began to race. Like a lot of Texas men, Ryder called all females "darlin'," whether they were one or one hundred. He had called her that from the first time they met and she had never given it a second thought. But this time there was something about the tone of his voice and the look in his eyes that made his use of the word extremely personal. This time, he actually meant it as an endearment. And instead of upsetting her as it might have a week ago, it made her feel incredibly special.

Confused, she placed her hand in his while she tried to process what might be happening between them. He helped her to her feet, then leading her out onto the dance floor, took her in his arms and pulled her to him. Without thinking twice, she wrapped her arms around his waist and it felt like the most natural thing in the world to rest her head against his broad chest.

When they had danced at Sam and Bria's party, they had both been mindful to keep a respectable space between them, to keep things companionable. But tonight there wasn't anything platonic about the way Ryder held her or the way she leaned against him.

As they swayed in time to the music, it felt as if the world was reduced to just the two of them and she had never felt as content as she did at that moment. For the first time in longer than she cared to remember, she felt as if she was where she belonged. That in itself should have scared her as little else could. But it didn't. She knew without question that Ryder would never do anything to harm her, either emotionally or physically. He was her safe haven.

Not even the feel of his hardening body pressed snuggly to her stomach frightened her. Instead, it made her feel as if the blood in her veins had been turned to warm honey and created an aching feeling in the most feminine part of her.

"Are you doing okay?" Ryder whispered close to her ear. "I'm not scaring you, am I?"

For the past several nights as she lay in his arms, she'd felt his body harden with desire and not once had he tried to press for them to make love. Leaning back to look up at him, she shook her head. "I trust you more than I've ever trusted anyone...and I doubt there's anything about you that would frighten me."

When the song ended, he stared at her for endless seconds. "Do you want to stay and dance some more? Or do you think you're ready to go back to my camper?"

There was a spark of need in his eyes that stole her breath. If she hadn't already felt the evidence of his desire, the look in his dark green gaze would have been enough to let her know that he wanted her. And with sudden clarity, she realized he was asking if she was ready for more than just returning to his trailer for the night. He was asking if she was ready to make love with him.

She took a deep breath, then another as she searched his face. With Ryder she was safe and there wasn't a doubt in her mind that if she said she wasn't ready, he would accept her decision. But was that what she wanted?

"I think I am ready to leave," she finally said, nodding.

Ryder closed his eyes a moment, then giving her a kiss that caused her head to spin, he took her by the hand and led her through the crowd. "There's Nate with Jaron over there," she said, pointing toward the dessert table. "Didn't you say you wanted to talk to him?"

"Yeah, but taking Nate to task in front of a bunch of people isn't my style," Ryder replied, as they walked across the rodeo grounds toward the camping area. "I'll wait until I can get him alone tomorrow before I chew on his sorry hide." He raised her hand to his mouth to kiss it. "Besides, I have other things on my mind right now."

When they reached his fifth wheel trailer, he unlocked the door, then helped her up the steps. The deluxe camper had more amenities than any hotel room and she could understand why Ryder preferred taking his accommodations with him. It truly was a home away from home. And a very luxurious one at that.

When he closed the door and secured the lock, he turned and immediately reached for her. "You do know I was asking if you felt ready to try making love again?" he asked, raining tiny kisses along the side of her neck.

His warm breath feathering over her skin sent shivers of excitement coursing the length of her and caused her knees to feel as if they were made of rubber. "Y-yes."

"I don't want you to feel rushed, Summer." He reached up to cup her face in his hands. "Are you sure?"

She nodded. "Yes."

His smile sent her temperature soaring. "If at any time you need to slow down or want to call a halt to things, tell me."

"I will."

Lowering his head, he gave her a kiss that sent tiny electric charges skipping over her nerve endings and caused heat to gather in her lower belly. Then, without a word, he took her by the hand and led her up the steps to the bedroom at the front of the camper.

"Aren't you going to turn on the light?" she asked when he knelt to remove her boots, then pulled off his.

"Not unless you want me to." His low, sexy tone caused her insides to feel as if they had been turned to warm pudding. "I want whatever makes you the most at ease with what we're doing."

She nodded as he wrapped his arms around her and hugged her close. "I think I'm good with the light off… for now."

"That's fine, darlin'." He kissed his way from her cheek, down her neck to the fluttering pulse at the base of her throat. "I'm going to take my clothes off first," he murmured against her skin. "Then I'll take off yours."

She briefly wondered why he was telling her everything he was about to do. Then it dawned on her that Ryder was making sure there were no surprises, as well as giving her the opportunity to stop him if her insecurities got the better of her. Her chest tightened with emotion at the lengths he was going to in order to help her overcome her fears.

Neither of them spoke as he removed his shirt and jeans, then reached for the pearl buttons on the front of her pink silk blouse. When his fingers brushed her collarbone as he worked the tiny disks free, she shivered. No other man's touch had ever caused her to feel the excitement or anticipation that Ryder's did. And she knew as surely as she knew her own name that no other man's touch ever would.

Her heart skipped several beats and she struggled to take a breath. Was she beginning to fall for him?

It went without saying that for the past few years she had been closer to him than she had been with any other man. And there was no doubt that she was extremely fond of him. But what she felt now was different and went beyond mere friendship.

"Darlin', I'm going to take off your blouse and unfasten your bra," he whispered, causing her to abandon her unsettling speculation.

When he slowly brushed the pink silk from her shoulders, then released the front clasp of her bra to slide the straps down her arms, he gently pulled her to him. The slight abrasion of his hair-roughened flesh against her overly sensitive nipples sent a need like nothing she had ever known coursing through her.

"O-oh…m-my," she stammered, wrapping her arms around his waist when her knees threatened to give way.

"Are you still doing okay?" he asked, kissing her bare shoulder as he reached between them to unsnap her jeans and slowly slide them down her thighs.

"Mmm…yes," she managed as she kicked the denim aside.

Waves of heat coursed from the top of her head to the tips of her toes when he wrapped his arms around her and covered her mouth with his. His firm lips moved over hers with such tenderness she thought she just might melt into a puddle at his feet. But when he coaxed her to open for him, the feel of his tongue as he stroked hers, the tender care he took as he explored her thoroughly, caused the heat inside of her to tighten into a deep coil of need.

The feeling intensified when he ran his hands down her back to cup her bottom and pull her into the cradle of his hips. The only barriers separating them were his cotton underwear and her lace panties.

"You feel so…good, darlin'." His tone was raspy and it sounded as if he had as much trouble drawing in oxygen as she was having. "Do you need for me to slow down?"

"N-no. I'm fine."

"I'm going to take the rest of our clothes off," he said, raining tiny kisses from her forehead to her chin.

Unable to make her vocal cords work, she simply nodded.

Ryder quickly pushed his boxer briefs down his long legs and kicked them aside, then reaching out, placed his hands at her waist and slowly slid his fingers under the elastic at her waist. Her breath caught at the slight abrasion of his calloused palms skimming over her hips and down her thighs as he lowered her panties.

Stepping out of them, she could hear the beating

of her own heart when he drew her to him. The sudden heat of his hard masculine flesh against her softer feminine skin sent a shock wave of desire all the way through her.

She had expected a moment of panic, but it never came. There was nothing frightening about feeling Ryder's body aligned with hers. Having her breasts crushed against his chest, feeling his hard, hot arousal snug against her lower stomach only caused the need inside of her to intensify.

"Why don't we lie down?" he suggested, swinging her up in his arms to carry her over to the bed. He placed her in the middle of the mattress as if she was a precious gift, then stretched out beside her. "I want you to be completely comfortable with everything we do, Summer." When she started to tell him that she was, he placed his index finger to her lips. "That's why I'm only going to take things so far. I'll make sure we're both ready to make love, then I'm going to let you take control."

"What do you mean?" she asked, confused.

Giving her a kiss hot enough to melt metal, he lightly touched her cheek. "I've seen you flinch a couple of times when I lean over you to kiss you good-night. I think you'll feel more at ease if you're the one on top of me instead of the other way around."

What he said was true. She still felt extremely vulnerable lying flat on her back.

"You don't mind?"

His low chuckle sent a wave of goose bumps over her entire body. "Darlin', you know I'm not an insecure man." She could just make out his wide grin in the darkened room. "Lovin' is lovin' whether I'm on bottom, on top or standing on my head."

Summer smiled. "That last position might be a little difficult."

Shrugging, he brushed her lips with his. "If that's what it takes to make you happy, then I'd give it my best shot."

Her heart swelled with emotion. "Ryder McClain, you're a very special man," she whispered, touching his lean cheek with her fingertips.

"Nah, I'm just a guy trying to help out his best friend," he said, running is hands over her bare back.

His calloused palms felt absolutely wonderful on her sensitized skin, but having him mention their friendship bothered her. And she wasn't entirely certain why. But as he continued to touch her, she gave up trying to pin down the reason she found it unsettling. At the moment, having Ryder's hands on her bare skin was creating far too many delicious sensations within her to concentrate on anything but the way he was making her feel.

When he lowered his lips to hers, she gave herself up to the mastery of his kiss and forgot about anything but the man holding her to him. As his mouth moved over hers, he slid his hand from her back to the underside of her breast, then cupping her, used his thumb to gently chafe the hardened tip. Tiny electric sparks skipped over every part of her and she couldn't have stopped her moan of pleasure if she'd tried.

"Does that feel good, Summer?" he asked, raining

kisses down her neck to her collarbone, then the valley between her breasts.

"Y-yes."

He continued to tease her with his thumb for a moment before kissing his way down the slope of her breast to take her into his mouth. His tongue against her tight flesh caused stars to burst behind her closed eyes and she was certain that if he continued much longer she would surely burn to a cinder.

"Y-you're driving me…crazy," she gasped.

"Darlin', it's only going to get better," he murmured as he moved to take her hand in his. Guiding her to him, he whispered, "I want you to touch me. I want you to see that there's nothing threatening about a man's body."

Doing as he commanded, she tentatively ran her palm over his hard flesh, then the softness below. She felt him shudder with need, but he didn't stop her exploration and made no demands of her.

"Now I'm going to touch you," he said, his tone tight, but nonthreatening.

When he found her, the coil inside her lower body tightened to an almost unbearable ache. "P-please, Ryder."

"What do you want, Summer?"

"You."

Giving her a quick kiss, he rolled to his back and pulled her on top of him. "I'm all yours, darlin'."

True to his word, he was handing her control and making sure she wasn't threatened by his much larger body hovering over hers, pinning her down, trapping her. His concessions caused a deep emotion she didn't dare identify to fill her chest as she straddled his lean hips.

When he helped her guide him to her, she closed her eyes as she slowly took him in. She didn't think she had ever felt more complete as she did at that moment. It was as if she had finally found a part of herself that she hadn't even realized was missing.

Placing his hands at her hips, he helped her set an easy pace as she began to rock against him. Her body quickly responded to being at one with him and all too soon she felt herself reaching for the completion they both sought.

"I'm going to touch you again, darlin'," Ryder said, sliding his hand between them.

The moment he stroked the tiny nub of sensation, the tight coil inside of her set her free and wave after wave of intense pleasure flowed through her. A moment later she felt Ryder go completely still, then with a low, raspy groan he wrapped his arms around her and released his sperm deep inside of her.

Collapsing on top of him, Summer felt as if their souls had touched and she knew in that moment why his calling her his friend bothered her. Ryder was more than her friend, he was the man she was falling for.

Seven

The following morning, Ryder watched Summer from across the pressroom as she sat in on an interview a reporter from a national magazine was doing with Nate. A top contender for the Champion All-Around Cowboy title, his brother's outgoing personality and quick wit were exactly what the rodeo association was looking for to promote their upcoming national finals.

But as proud as Ryder was of his brother and his accomplishments, his main focus was on Summer. She was amazing and without a doubt the most captivating, desirable woman he had ever met. What he couldn't get over was why he had been immune to her charms before. How could he have been so blind?

When they had returned to his camper from the dance last night, he'd half expected for her to decide that she wasn't yet ready to make love. And although he hadn't looked forward to it, he had been fully prepared to endure a shower cold enough to freeze the balls off a pool table.

But Summer had surprised him and they had shared the most mind-blowing night of lovemaking he had ever experienced. He had done everything he could think of to make her feel as comfortable as possible, and with the exception of wanting the light off, she had been fine. She had even seemed to forget that they were making love for the purpose of conceiving a baby. For that matter so had he. All he'd been able to think about was the woman in his bed and how she excited him in ways he could have never imagined.

He frowned as he mulled that over. When had he lost sight of wanting to help Summer with her request of having a baby and simply started wanting her?

He had come to terms with the notion that their friendship had been permanently altered. That had happened the first time he had kissed her. In all of his thirty-three years, he'd never tasted lips so sweet or as soft as Summer's.

But what bothered him the most about the whole damn thing was that he could very well be helping her get over her fears of intimacy only to have her meet another man she decided she could settle down with. Then where would he be? He would not only lose his best friend, he would forfeit the right to make love to the most exhilarating woman he had ever known.

He tried to tell himself that it didn't matter since they really had no future together. Besides the fact that he didn't want to saddle any woman with his past, how could he tell Summer that the man she thought had such a high degree of integrity was a miserable fraud?

The thought had Ryder getting up from the chair he had been sitting in to amble out of the pressroom into the hallway. What the hell was wrong with him?

He wasn't interested in taking their relationship any further than they already had. So why did he have a knot the size of a football twisting his gut at the thought of Summer finding out about his past or moving on with her life in the arms of another man?

"Bro, you look like you got hold of a persimmon that wasn't quite ripe," Nate said, striding up to him as he walked out of the pressroom. "Are you all right?"

"Yeah, but you're not going to be if you pull another stunt like the one you did yesterday," Ryder shot back. It was easier to focus on his brother's lack of concentration yesterday in the bull riding event than it was to think about what he could never have with Summer. "If your head isn't in the game, don't climb on the back of another bull and risk getting into a wreck that might get you hurt real bad or worse."

Nate had the good sense not to argue. "I'm sorry about yesterday. But don't worry, bro. I've got things under control now." He grinned. "You know it's hard to keep me down for very long."

"Already turning on the charm with another unsuspecting woman, are you?" Ryder asked, relieved to see that Nate was more himself than he had been the day before.

"Nope." Nate shrugged. "I've decided to take a break

from the ladies for a while and focus on winning the All-Around."

Ryder frowned. Lane had been right; there was a lot more going on with Nate than a case of wounded pride. He must have fallen pretty hard for that nurse he'd been seeing if he was willingly giving up female companionship in favor of a rodeo title.

Before he could caution his brother further, Summer's hand on his arm stopped him. "Ryder, when you get time, I need to talk with you before the events start," she said, giving him a smile that caused his jeans to feel like they were a couple of sizes too small in the stride.

"Sure thing, darlin'." He turned back to Nate. "You know I'll have your back out there this afternoon. But remember what I said and pay attention to what you're doing."

"Will do," Nate said before he walked down the hall toward the training room.

"Is he all right?" Summer asked.

"I think so." Ryder put his arm around her shoulders and started back toward the pressroom. "Now what do you need to talk to me about?"

When they entered the empty room, she closed the door behind them. "I just wanted to tell you to be safe out there this afternoon," she said, wrapping her arms around his waist.

Hugging her close, he nodded. "I'll make sure of it. I have plans for tonight."

"Really?"

He lowered his head to brush her perfect coral lips

with his. "Oh yeah. I think we should skip the dance this evening and go to bed early."

"You're already sleepy?" The twinkle in her blue eyes indicated that she knew better.

"Darlin', when we go to bed tonight, I seriously doubt that sleeping will be on either of our minds," he murmured, kissing her until they both gasped for breath. "Are you doing all right? You should have woke me when you got up this morning."

"I couldn't be better," she said, rising on tiptoes to kiss his chin. "And you were sleeping so peacefully, I couldn't bring myself to wake you. Your job is so much more physically demanding than mine, I wanted you to rest."

"So now you're taking care of me?" Other than his brothers and his foster father, Hank, no one had ever bothered to look after his well-being.

She looked thoughtful for a moment, then nodded. "You're so busy watching out for everyone else, you need someone to take care of you."

Before he could respond, a knock on the pressroom door caused Summer to pull from his arms. When the door opened, a man holding a microphone like it was some kind of trophy walked in. "Excuse me, but would either of you know where I could find the PR guy?"

The man inquiring looked to be somewhere around his own age and a little too slick and sure of himself. "Who wants to know?" Ryder asked, taking an instant dislike to the man.

"I'm Chip Marx from Live Eye News," the fellow answered, managing to look down his nose at Ryder even though he was a good six inches shorter than Ryder's six-foot-two-inch frame.

He acted like they should immediately recognize him and his name. Besides finding the guy irritating as hell, it didn't mean squat to Ryder.

"I'm Summer Patterson, the regional rodeo association's public relations director," she said, extending her hand. "What can I do for you, Mr. Marx?"

The little weasel's demeanor changed immediately. "Well, now, this is a pleasant surprise," Marx said, flashing a bleach-toothed grin as he took her hand. He didn't shake it, but continued to hold on to it. "I can tell I'm going to enjoy doing this story after all."

Ryder watched Summer tug her hand free before reaching for a copy of the press release she had prepared. "Here's the information you'll need. If you have any questions, let me know. Since this is the last day and most of the cowboys are already getting ready to compete, I doubt that I'd be able to arrange an interview with one of them." She nodded cordially at him. "They usually take off to make the trip to the next rodeo as soon as the events are over with on the last day."

"Oh, this isn't for this week's dog and pony show," he said, laughing as he shook his head. "I'm here to do an advance story on the rodeo next week down in New Mexico. I'd also like for my cameraman to get some footage of the cowboys doing whatever it is they do."

"All right," Summer said, sounding reluctant. Ryder could tell she didn't like the guy any more than he did. "I'll arrange for a couple of seats in the VIP area. It's closer to the arena action. You should get some pretty good footage of the events from there."

"We would rather follow you around and get some of the behind-the-scenes stories." Marx pointed to his cameraman just outside the door. "He can get some video of the animals as well as the cowboys preparing for their rides."

"That isn't going to happen, Mr. Marx." Ryder had seen that look of determination on Summer's face before. She was the one calling the shots and wasn't about to let the guy dictate to her what he was going to do. "For one thing, this is a rodeo. It's not a 'dog and pony show.' And for another, you don't tell me what you're going to do. I tell you. The reason for that is to ensure your safety as well as that of the crew behind the chutes. Now if you can accept those terms, I'll be more than happy to arrange for you to get your story. If you can't, then our business here is finished."

Ryder had never been more proud of her. He had seen her deal with pushy reporters before, and he could have told Marx his dictatorial tactics wouldn't work. But watching her tell the man in no uncertain terms that she was in charge was a lot more enjoyable.

The guy didn't look the least bit happy, but apparently realizing Summer wasn't going to budge, he shrugged. "Well, I suppose we could get whatever footage we need from the VIP section." He flashed his practiced grin. "Would it be possible to get an interview with you after the events are over?"

"That could probably be arranged," she answered slowly. "But it will have to be brief."

"That's fine," Marx said. "I'll get what I can today and then set up something with you for next week's rodeo."

"I'll call the VIP attendant and have your seats waiting for you," Summer said, dismissing the man.

Marx looked like he would like to say more, but instead turned and walked out without so much as a thank-you. "Someone needs to teach that jerk some manners," Ryder said darkly.

"I've dealt with his type before," she replied, shrugging as she reached for her cell phone.

Ryder checked his watch. "While you make that call, I'll go get changed." He gave her a quick kiss. "I'll see you in a little while, darlin'."

"Be careful," she said, looking a little worried.

"Always am," he assured her.

During the bull riding event, Summer was too nervous to watch Ryder play tag with a ton of bovine fury. It was completely ridiculous, considering she had seen him do it almost every weekend for the past three years. But that was before he'd held her, kissed her, made love to her.

Busying herself with clearing out the pressroom to keep her mind off what was happening between them, an ominous announcement over the loud speaker caused a chill to snake up her spine and sent her running toward the area behind the chutes. The medical trainers were calling for an ambulance to enter the arena. That meant someone had been injured. And it was serious if they weren't bringing the rider back to the training room for evaluation before sending him on to the hospital.

Searching for Ryder, her heart felt as if it stopped beating completely until she spotted him kneeling beside a rider lying facedown in the loose dirt on the arena floor. Weak with relief, she looked around to make sure the fallen rider wasn't one of his brothers.

"Who is it?" she asked the chute boss.

He named one of the younger cowboys, then added, "The kid fell forward on Sidewinder's first jump out of the gate and knocked himself out. If it hadn't been for Ryder, that boy would have been a goner for sure. As soon as he hit the dirt, Ryder fell on top of him to protect him from getting kicked or stomped."

"Is Ryder okay?" she asked, holding her breath. On several different occasions she had seen him put himself in jeopardy to protect a cowboy who had no chance of protecting himself.

"I think he might have been shook-up when Sidewinder butted him in the side, but that's about it," the man answered. "He might be a little sore in the morning, but his Kevlar vest should have kept him from getting a couple of cracked ribs."

Once she learned that the young cowboy had regained consciousness and would be transported to the hospital for a CT scan and observation, the bull riding resumed and Summer had to wait until the rest of the event was concluded before she could approach Ryder. It felt like an eternity. She needed to talk to him and see for herself that he was all right.

As she impatiently paced the area behind the chutes,

she tried to figure out why she was so anxious…why she was more upset by his bravery than she had ever been before. She had always known it was his job to put himself between the cowboys and the dangerous bulls. He was one of the best and hundreds of men had Ryder to thank for saving them from serious injury and, in some cases, for saving their lives.

But the stakes had been raised and she had a feeling she knew why. She had always been fond of him, but this time she was seeing his acts of heroism through the eyes of a woman who was falling harder for him than she had any other man.

Summer took a bolstering breath as she acknowledged her feelings. She had suspected her feelings for him had developed into something much deeper than mere friendship after they made love last night, but she had refused to think about it. She had told herself not to jump to conclusions—that it was probably just the afterglow of their lovemaking she was experiencing. She knew now that her feelings went far deeper than that.

"Darlin', if you don't stop pacing, you're going to wear the dirt down to bedrock," Ryder said from behind her.

Turning, she hurried over to him and threw her arms around his neck. "Are you all right?"

His arms immediately closed around her. "I'm fine. Old Sidewinder just gave me a couple of nudges to tell me hello."

Suddenly angered by his casual dismissal of what had been a very serious situation, she stepped away from him. "Don't you dare say it was nothing, Ryder

McClain! You could have been hurt or worse. What if that stupid bull had stepped on you?"

"Whoa! Where's this coming from?" He looked confused. "You know it's my job to save riders. Hell, you've seen me do it at least a hundred times over the past few years."

"That was before," she protested, knowing she was overreacting but unable to stop herself.

He frowned. "Before what?"

She couldn't tell him that she had fallen for him. "We'll talk about this tonight," she said before turning to walk back to the pressroom. "I have to get things packed up and ready for next weekend."

"I'll help you," he said, falling into step beside her.

Out of the corner of her eye, she saw him glance at her several times as if trying to figure out what had gotten into her. She knew beyond a shadow of doubt what the problem was, but how was she supposed to explain that for the first time, instead of seeing him as a friend and coworker putting himself in danger, she had been watching through the eyes of a woman who was on the verge of falling head over heels in love with him? She hadn't fully come to terms with it herself and he probably wasn't expecting to hear it anyway.

"Did you get the interview with that little weasel over with?" he asked.

"Oh rats! I forgot all about that." How could a day start out to be so good, then turn into a royal headache so fast?

When they entered the pressroom, she sighed. Chip Marx was waiting for her.

"I was beginning to wonder if you were going to stand me up," he said, his smile barely hiding his impatience.

"I'm sure you can understand that when we have a rider taken away by ambulance it's a serious matter," she said, doing her best not to lose her temper with the man. "My first priority is to get accurate information about the cowboy's injuries and assess whether I need to notify his family or make a statement to the media."

"Of course." He didn't look at all as if he understood or cared. "Why don't we do a dinner interview? That way I'll have your undivided attention."

When Summer glanced at Ryder, she caught her breath. He looked furious. And she couldn't blame him. She was angered by the man's insensitivity, as well. He hadn't even bothered to ask if the injured rider was going to be all right.

"I'm sorry, but I won't have time to talk with you after all, Mr. Marx."

"Please, call me Chip," he said, his tone suggestive.

He gave her a grin that she was sure he'd stood in front of a mirror practicing—probably for years. If he thought it would win her over, he was sadly mistaken.

"As I told you, I don't have time…Chip." She hadn't meant for his name to come out sounding as if she said a dirty word, but at the moment she really didn't care.

"You have to eat anyway," he insisted. "It might as well be with me."

She'd just as soon dine with a snake. "Thank you, but I meant it when I said I don't have time. Now, if you'll excuse me, I have to get the rest of the pressroom shut down and ready to move on to the venue in New Mexico."

The man didn't seem to grasp the concept that she wanted nothing more to do with him and, stepping forward, took hold of her arm. "Surely you can—"

"The lady says she doesn't have time," Ryder interrupted, moving in to wrap his hand around the man's wrist and remove it from her arm. "Now, I suggest you take Ms. Patterson at her word and find another story."

She had only heard Ryder use that deadly tone one other time. The night she had told him about being raped.

Ryder must have applied pressure to the man's wrist because Chip Marx let out a yelp and winced in pain. "You can't do this." He glared at his cameraman. "Don't just stand there! Get footage of this. I'll need it when I sue this goat roper for assault."

The cameraman glanced from Marx to Ryder, then back to Marx. "You're on your own, Chip," he said, turning to walk out of the room. "I didn't see a thing."

Summer had never seen Ryder look as dangerous as he did at that moment and she couldn't say she blamed the cameraman for bailing on the arrogant reporter. Calling a cowboy a "goat roper" was extremely insulting and not at all wise when the cowboy in question had a vise-grip hold on your arm.

"It's all right, Ryder," she said, hoping to defuse the situation. "He was just leaving, weren't you, Mr. Marx?"

Before the reporter could answer, Ryder nodded toward the door. "You'd better take her advice, Marx. Otherwise, you'll force me to kick your ass. Since I'm still wearing cleats, something tells me that would make the experience doubly painful. And just so we have things straight…I'd better not catch you bothering Ms. Patterson again." Turning the man loose, he finished, "Because if you do, you'll be picking your bleached teeth up off the floor. Are we clear on that?"

His face beet-red, Chip Marx turned to rush from the room. But apparently as stupid as he was arrogant, he turned back for one parting shot. "This isn't over."

"Yes, it is," Ryder said, taking a step forward. The man fled as if he was being chased by the devil.

"Thank you, Ryder, but I'm sure I could have handled that situation myself," she said, reaching for a stack of brochures. She wasn't at all sure, but she didn't want him to know just how vulnerable she had felt.

He shook his head. "I know you're capable of taking care of most things like this, and I'm fine with that. But when that lowlife put his hand on you…" His voice trailed off for a moment before he took a deep breath and cleared his throat. "I'm not going to apologize because I'm not sorry I stepped in." Turning, he walked to the door. "And just so you know. As long as I have breath in my body, no man will ever treat you the way that bastard just tried to do and get away with it."

Long after Ryder left, Summer stared at the empty doorway. For the past several years, she had dealt with pushy reporters who thought they could bully or charm her into doing what they wanted and she'd never had a problem putting them in their place. But until today, none of them had ever crossed the line and put his hands on her.

She shuddered as she finished packing the small container with brochures and picked it up to leave. The only man's touch that didn't make her want to shrink away in revulsion, the only man she ever wanted to touch her, was Ryder.

Her heart skipped a beat as she acknowledged her feelings. She had tried to avoid putting a name to how her relationship with him had evolved. Acting as if they were a couple was only supposed to have been roles they were playing for the benefit of their coworkers and his brothers in preparation for the baby they were going to have together. But there was no sense in evading any longer what she knew in her heart was true. Even if she didn't feel she could reveal to him how she really felt, she could at least admit it to herself. She had fallen in love with Ryder McClain.

Ryder leaned up against the side of the arena, waiting on Summer. After leaving the pressroom, he had decided to make sure that Marx was long gone and wouldn't give her any more trouble. And he had no doubt that if given the chance, the man was stupid enough to try putting the moves on her again. Pushy little weasels like Marx thought they were God's gift to women and couldn't get it through their thick heads that they weren't adored by every female they came in contact with.

He sighed heavily. The last thing he had wanted was for her to see him lose his temper. And he'd been damned close to doing just that. Fortunately, for her sake as well as Marx's, Ryder had been able to keep a tight rein on his control.

He couldn't have cared less that the man had insulted him. As far as he was concerned, Marx's opinion of him didn't matter one way or the other. But when he grabbed Summer's arm, Ryder had damned near come unglued. It had taken every ounce of restraint he had in him to keep from knocking the jerk into the middle of next week. Unfortunately, he couldn't guarantee that the next time he would be able to stop himself. And that bothered him almost as much as Marx putting his hand on Summer.

"I thought you left to go back to the camper to shower and change clothes," Summer said, stopping in front of him as she left the arena.

"Nope." He shoved away from the wall to take the small box she carried. "I thought I'd stick around to carry this for you."

As they walked across the fairgrounds toward his camper, they fell silent. He hated the awkwardness and figured she was still upset that he hadn't let her handle Marx on her own. But he had told her the truth. As long as he was around, no one would ever lay an unwelcomed hand on her.

Stowing the container in the outside cargo area of the fifth wheel, he unlocked the door and helped her up the steps. "As soon as I shower and get changed, we can go to the barbecue if you'd like."

"I thought you wanted to stay in this evening," she said, frowning. "I was going to make some sandwiches for us."

"After that run-in with Marx, I wasn't sure you'd want—" Stopping himself, Ryder shook his head. "Never mind. Whatever you want to do is fine with me."

She stared at him for several seconds, then surprising the hell out of him, moved closer to wrap her arms around him. His arms automatically closed around her to hold her close.

"Today was the first time since I started this job that I felt threatened," she said, her voice trembling. "I didn't want to admit it, but when Chip Marx took hold of my arm, I was actually afraid."

"Summer, I was right there with you." Ryder leaned back to look down at her. "You've got to know there's no way in hell I'd ever let him do anything to you."

She nodded. "I know that. And I wasn't upset with you for stepping in to stop him. I was mad at myself for allowing him to frighten me." She shuddered against him. "But he gives me the creeps."

"Forget about Marx. He's not worth the time and trouble to give him a second thought." He kissed the tip of her nose. "Now, while I go take a shower, why don't you make those sandwiches."

"I can do that," she said, her sweet smile sending his hormones racing around like the steel bearings in a pinball machine.

He swallowed hard and forced himself to climb the steps to the upper level of the camper. "I'll only be a few minutes."

Showering in record time, he wrapped a towel around his waist and walked into the bedroom. He stopped short at the sight of Summer wearing nothing but his T-shirt and her panties.

Her cheeks turned pink as she grabbed her robe and held it in front of her. “I thought your shower would take a little longer.”

“Nope.”

“Since we aren’t going out…I thought I would change into something more comfortable,” she said hesitantly. Her gaze drifted to his bare chest and she reached out to lightly touch the small white scar just below his left pectoral muscle. “I didn’t notice this the other night when I put ointment on the scratches. What happened?”

Ryder clenched his teeth at the surge of heat caused by her fingertips caressing his skin. “I got hooked by a bull about ten years ago.”

“You weren’t wearing your Kevlar vest?” she asked, stepping closer. She rested her palm over the scar and he felt like he’d been branded.

The light herbal scent of her hair and her soft touch caused his body to harden and he had to clear his throat before he could answer. “It didn’t happen at a rodeo. I was helping Hank move one of his herds and a bull got loose. When it started to charge him, I figured I had a better chance of dodging it than he did because I could move a little faster.”

She raised her eyes to meet his and the spark of desire he detected in the blue depths robbed him of breath. “You’re a true hero, Ryder McClain.”

Taking the robe from her other hand, he tossed it aside then took her in his arms and pulled her close. “Summer, I’m flattered that you think I’m such a nice guy. But I didn't do anything more than any other man would have done in the same situation."

"You're my hero," she insisted, gazing up at him.

As they stared at each other, Ryder felt guilty as hell. He didn't deserve her admiration, but he couldn't tell her that the man she held in such high regard wasn't what she thought he was.

To distract her from saying something else that would only end up making him feel even worse than he already did, he lowered his mouth to hers. The sweet taste of her lips quickly had him forgetting about anything but the woman in his arms and how much he wanted her. Considering that the only things keeping him from having all of her against him was the towel around his waist and the thin cotton T-shirt and panties she had on, it was no wonder his lower body had come to full alert.

When she raised her arms to wrap them around his neck and leaned more fully against him, he half expected her to bolt at the feel of his arousal pressed to her soft stomach. But to his immense satisfaction, instead of pulling away, her lips parted on a sigh. Encouraged by her response, he deepened the kiss to coax and tease.

"Darlin'…I think…we'd better…slow down," he said when he broke the kiss to nibble his way along her jaw to the delicate shell of her ear. "I give you my word that nothing is going to happen unless you want it to, but I'm hotter than a two-dollar pistol on Saturday night and want you more now than I've ever wanted anything in my entire life."

"But it's not…dark yet," she said, looking a little unsure despite the blush of desire coloring her cheeks.

Ryder laughed, releasing some of the tension that gripped him. "Our bodies will fit together just as well in the daylight as they do in the dark."

"I'm well aware of that, cowboy," she retorted, giving him a look that suggested he might be a little simple-minded. "But when it's dark it's not as easy to see…" Her voice trailed off and her cheeks turned a deeper shade of pink.

He could have told her that although his T-shirt covered her from neck to midthigh, it was still thin enough for him to see the silhouette of her delightful curves and the shape and size of her perfect breasts. But he wisely kept that bit of information to himself. Although she had become a little more comfortable with intimacy in the past few days, she still had a couple of lingering issues.

"Do you still want to make a baby with me, Summer?" he said huskily.

"Yes. But—"

"And do you still trust me?" he asked.

She nodded. "Of course."

He gave her a quick kiss. "I give you my word on this, darlin'. I won't see any more of you than what you want me to see."

Eight

Ryder's heated look sent a wave of goose bumps shimmering over her skin as he swung her up into his arms, then placing her in the middle of the bed, reached for the towel at his waist. Scrunching her eyes shut, Summer waited until she felt him stretch out beside her and pull the sheet over them.

Opening her eyes, she turned onto her side to face him. "You certainly aren't shy about your body."

"Nope." He smiled. "Most guys aren't hung up with modesty issues like women are."

"I wonder why?"

He reached out to take her in his arms. "Do you really want to talk about the lack of inhibitions in men right now?"

The hunger in his eyes stole her breath and she suddenly wasn't sure what he had asked her. When he covered her mouth with his, she decided it really didn't matter. All she could think about was the way Ryder was making her feel.

Less than a week ago, she had thought she was immune to desire and passion. But Ryder's kiss, his gentle touch and the concessions he had made for her peace of mind, had not only convinced her that her trust was well placed, it created a need in her stronger than she had ever dreamed possible.

Parting her lips, she welcomed him slipping his tongue inside to explore her with a thoroughness that sent a delicious warmth coursing throughout her body. But when he slowly glided his hand down her thigh to the hem of the T-shirt she was wearing and lifted it as he brought his hand back up to cup her breast, the heat inside of her coiled into a pool of deep need.

"Look at me, Summer," he whispered close to her ear. When her eyes met his, he smiled. "I'm going to take off this shirt and your panties now, darlin'."

A shiver of anticipation made its way up her spine as he swept the T-shirt up and over her head, then reached for the elastic at her waist. Not once did his gaze waver from hers and by the time the scrap of satin and lace was sent to join the shirt over the side of the bed, she realized that Ryder had kept his word. He hadn't so much as glanced at her body. She loved him even more for his integrity and the understanding he had shown for her self-consciousness.

Her heart skipped a beat and she closed her eyes as she felt her love for him blossom. She was no longer making love with her best friend in order to have a baby. She was making love with her soul mate—the man she had fallen hopelessly in love with. She had even forgotten all about their coming together for her to become pregnant.

But apparently he hadn't lost sight of the reason behind the intimacy they had shared last night and were about to share again. Why else would he have mentioned it?

She sighed. If he was still focused on their goal, that meant his feelings for her hadn't developed into anything more than what they had always felt for each other—a deep abiding friendship and a wealth of mutual respect.

Before she could give the matter more thought and come to terms with the fact that Ryder might not ever feel anything more for her, his fingers grazed her cheek. "What's wrong, Summer?"

When she opened her eyes, he was propped up on one elbow, staring down at her, his expression reflecting his concern. Reaching up, she cupped his lean cheek with her palm. "How could anything be wrong?" she asked, evading his question. "My best friend and I are about to make a baby."

He stared at her for endless seconds, as if trying to determine the real reason behind her heartfelt sigh, then lowering his lips to hers, gave her a kiss so tender it caused tears to flood her eyes. Ryder might be a giant compared to her petite frame, but he was the most gentle man she had ever known.

As he deepened the kiss to tease and explore her with feathery flicks of his tongue, his hand moved along her side and down her thigh. Caressing the back of her knee for a moment, he skimmed his palm back up to the apex of her thighs. Parting her, his touch caused her body to hum with an energy that threatened to consume her.

Lost in the delightful sensations he aroused in the most feminine part of her, it took a moment for her to realize that he was lifting her leg to drape it over his hips. "Ryder?"

"We're going to make love face-to-face, Summer. You need to see that it's me making love to you, not some selfish bastard taking what he wants." He kissed her bare shoulder. "I want to watch the moment I bring you pleasure…and I want you to see me when you help me find mine."

Her chest swelled with emotion. Ryder was an incredibly compassionate man. He had vowed to help her get over her intimacy issues, and he was doing everything he could to reassure her that she was safe in his arms.

Before she could find her voice to tell him how much his consideration meant to her, he moved to align their hips and she felt his blunt tip poised to enter her. His green eyes darkened as he captured her gaze with his and he slowly pressed forward. Feeling herself become one with the man she loved, seeing the tender passion on his handsome face as he filled her was utterly breathtaking.

With their eyes locked, he slowly began to move within her. Neither spoke as their bodies communicated in ways no words could ever express and all too soon, Summer felt the coil of need inside of her begin to tighten as she moved closer to the pinnacle. Her body ached to hold on, to prolong the moment of being one with Ryder, but he deepened his thrusts and she suddenly felt herself trembling from the pleasure rushing through every part of her. Unable to stop herself, she closed her eyes as she savored the exquisite feelings of unbridled fulfillment.

Ryder suddenly went completely still for a moment. Opening her eyes to focus on the man she loved with all her heart and soul, Summer watched as he found the satisfaction of his own release. A groan rumbled up from deep in Ryder's chest as his big body shuddered against her and he filled her with his essence.

For the next several days when he wasn't in the open-air arena at the fairgrounds just outside of Albuquerque saving some poor rodeo rider's hide from being stomped on by a bull, Ryder found himself hanging around the press tent. He liked watching Summer do her job. She was nothing short of a miracle worker when it came to dealing with schedule changes and any number of other problems that arose at the last minute. He had watched her put together press kits and arrange a goodwill trip for some of the cowboys to a children's wing in one of the hospitals, in addition to coordinating interviews with the media so they could get their stories and photographs without being in harm's way.

Walking up behind her, he wrapped his arms around her waist and pulled her back against him. "Do you have any idea just how incredible you are, Summer Patterson?"

"Incredibly tired is more like it," she sighed, leaning back against him. "I haven't been getting a lot of sleep lately."

He turned her to face him. "Is that a complaint?"

Her sweet smile sent his temperature sky high. "Not at all, cowboy. I've just recently discovered how relaxing nighttime activities can be."

Laughing out loud, Ryder pulled her to him for a quick hug. "We can always skip the barbecue and dance tonight and turn in early."

"I'm actually looking forward to the party," she said, snuggling closer. "After tonight I won't have to worry about the possibility of running into a certain pushy reporter who has a problem taking 'no' for an answer."

"Has old Chip contacted you?" he asked, hoping like hell the man had the good sense to look elsewhere for a story. He didn't like any man who tried to get a woman to bend to his will, but the behavior Chip Marx had displayed bordered on harassment and Ryder wasn't about to tolerate it.

"No, I haven't heard from Mr. Marx and I doubt that I will now. Since everything is drawing to a close today, he's missed his chance to find something to report." She rose up on tiptoe to kiss his lips. "Thanks to you, I'm pretty sure he got the message."

"He'd better," Ryder said, then reluctantly took a step back. "I need to go change and get ready to tango with a bunch of bovines."

"Be careful and save some of those dance moves for tonight," she said, smiling as she turned back to straighten a display of promotional items.

As he left the tent and headed toward the trailer, Ryder couldn't help but grin. Summer had conquered most of her intimacy issues, and although she was still hung up on how much they saw of each other in the bedroom, she seemed completely comfortable making love with him. In fact, she had even initiated their lovemaking last night.

His easy expression faded and he couldn't help but wonder what would happen once she became pregnant. Would he continue to have the privilege of holding her every night, to be able to make love to the most captivating woman he had ever met? Or would they try to return to the easy friendship they had enjoyed before?

He shook his head as he let himself into the trailer and gathered his bullfighting gear. He didn't see any way in hell they could go back. Not when he knew how responsive she was to his touch, how when they made love he felt like he had finally discovered the other half of himself.

Sucking in a sharp breath, he stood as still as a marble statue. Had he fallen in love with Summer? Was that why he couldn't imagine his life going on without the sweet intimacy they shared?

With his heart thumping against his ribs, he cursed his foolishness and finished getting ready to do his job. He wasn't in love with Summer. She was his best friend and the woman he was trying to make a baby with. He had the same needs as any other normal, red-blooded male and after a long dry spell without the softness of a woman, it was only natural that making love to her every night was influencing his emotions.

He stood up to leave the trailer and go back to the arena. And if he kept outlining all the reasons why he was starting to feel the way he did about Summer, he just might start to believe them.

Ryder held her hand as they walked to the pavilion where the after-rodeo barbecue and dance were being held. Truth be told, Summer didn't think she had ever been happier. Since beginning their physical relationship, she had started feeling like a woman again and not the skittish female who shuddered at the thought of being alone with a man. It was empowering and she loved the cowboy walking beside her for the special man he was and for helping her heal the emotional scars she hadn't thought she could ever overcome.

"I don't know what you're thinking, but it must be pretty nice," Ryder murmured, leaning down close to her ear in order to be heard above the live band.

"Why do you say that?" she asked, unwilling to reveal her feelings before she knew for certain he felt the same.

"Because you look like you know something nobody else knows and you can't wait to share it," he said with a wide grin.

"Maybe I do." She loved the intimate teasing and playfulness that had developed between them over the past couple of weeks.

"Want to let me in on the secret?" he asked, looking as if he already knew what she might be thinking.

"Not yet."

She actually had more than one secret, but she wasn't

going to jinx either one of them by talking about them too soon. She was certain that she loved Ryder and she would eventually tell him when the time was right. But her other secret was one that would take a trip to the drugstore and the purchase of an early pregnancy test to confirm. She was only a couple of days late, but due to the fact that her cycle had always been quite regular and she hadn't had any of the premenstrual symptoms she normally experienced, she was almost positive they had already been successful in conceiving.

"Let's dance," she said, tugging him toward the dance floor when the band started playing a slow tune.

When he took her in his arms, Summer leaned against him and realized that she was never more content than when they were holding each other. And knowing him the way she did, she had a feeling Ryder just might be feeling the same way.

"While I go get us a couple of drinks, why don't you find a table, darlin'?" he said when the dance ended.

Kissing his chin, she grinned. "You've got a deal, cowboy."

When she spotted an empty table in a secluded corner of the pavilion, Summer started toward it. She liked the idea of being able to talk with Ryder and not have to worry about being overheard. But as she made her way along the edge of the crowd, she stopped short when an imposing figure stepped out of the shadows and into her path.

"Well, imagine meeting you here," Chip Marx said, his speech slurred. He had obviously had too much to drink and, if the sarcastic expression on his face was any indication, he wasn't a very nice drunk.

"Good evening, Mr. Marx," she responded, attempting to step around him.

He caught her by the wrist to stop her. "Hey, where you going?"

A cold chill slithered up her spine. But she wasn't going to let him see that he was frightening her. Arrogant jerks like Marx fed on fear and intimidation. If she could keep from it, she refused to give him that kind of power over her.

"It's none of your business where I'm going," she said, pulling her arm back in an attempt to break his hold.

He tightened his grip and her hand began to ache from having the circulation cut off. "Where's your friend?" he asked, glancing around. "I'll bet you're not nearly as high-and-mighty when the goat roper isn't around."

"Number one, I don't appreciate you insulting Ryder," she said, stalling for time. Chip Marx was inching them away from the crowd and closer to the shadows where no one could see what he was up to. "And number two, he should be returning with our drinks at any moment. Do you really want him to see you with your hand on me again?"

"Too late," Ryder said from behind her.

A mixture of relief and dread coursed through her. She was relieved that Ryder had arrived before the man had a chance to drag her into the shadows, but if she had thought his voice sounded dangerous the first time

Chip Marx had grabbed her, it was nothing compared to the deadliness in his deep baritone now.

"Ryder, I'm sure Mr. Marx was leaving," she said, hoping to avoid a confrontation.

"No, I wasn't," Marx said, showing that he was every bit as stupid as she suspected. "And I'm not going to let the likes of him keep me from getting to know you better."

Marx suddenly released his hold on her and, shoving her to the side, took a swing at Ryder. Easily dodging the man's doubled fist, Ryder's punch was forceful, accurate and very effective. Chip Marx fell to the dirt like a discarded rag doll and as Ryder had promised the man the first time he grabbed her, two of his once sparkling white teeth, now bloody and broken, lay on the ground beside him.

Ryder immediately took her in his arms. "Are you all right?"

Nodding slowly, she hitched in a breath as she stared down at Chip Marx. She didn't like seeing anyone hurt, but she had no doubt that if Ryder hadn't arrived when he did, Marx would have dragged her off into the shadows and… She didn't even want to think about what he might have done.

"I was frightened, but I didn't want him to see it. I'm glad you showed up when you did." Glancing up, Summer wasn't prepared for the look of abject misery on Ryder's handsome face. "Are you all right?" When he remained silent as he continued to stare down at Marx's limp body, she started to become alarmed. "Ryder?"

It took a moment for him to finally look at her. "I

didn't want to have to do that," he said, his voice rough with emotion.

Summer shook her head. "He really didn't give you a lot of choice."

"We saw the whole thing and Summer's right, bro."

Looking up at the sound of the male voice, Summer was glad to see Nate and Jaron jogging toward them.

"It isn't your fault there's no cure for stupid," Jaron said, kneeling beside Marx. He took off his black Resistol and fanned it over Marx's face to help bring him around. "It was a case of punch or be punched, Ryder."

"I agree," an unfamiliar voice said. As Summer watched, a security guard hurried over to join them. "Are you all right, ma'am?"

"I'm fine," she answered.

"I saw the whole thing and it was self-defense. Plain and simple." The uniformed man shook his head as they watched Marx begin to stir. "When I saw him accost this little lady, I was trying to get over here to intervene, but I couldn't get through the crowd fast enough." The older man looked directly at Ryder. "To tell you the truth, I admire your restraint, son. If the bastard had grabbed my woman the way he did yours, I'd probably still be pounding on his worthless hide."

"We probably need to call the police and make a report," Ryder said, taking a deep breath. Nothing any of the other men had said seemed to be able to ease the morose expression on Ryder's face.

"Don't worry about it," the security guard said, pointing to a camera mounted on one of the pavilion rafters. "I've got the whole thing on tape and you can give me your name and where you can be reached in case the police get involved." He chuckled. "But it's my guess that once this fellow is fully conscious and he sees the video I'm going to show him, he won't be all that eager about getting the police in on this. If he does, he's going to be facing assault charges for manhandling the lady."

Once Ryder had given the guard the information he asked for, he turned to her. "Are you ready to go back to the trailer?"

Summer didn't have to think twice about her answer. "Yes."

Her concern increased when she glanced at Nate and Jaron. They looked just as concerned as she was.

"We'll talk to you when we meet up at the rodeo in Las Cruces a few days from now," Nate said, helping Jaron haul Chip Marx to his feet. "Hang in there, Ryder. You didn't have a choice."

As she and Ryder walked the short distance to the camping area, Summer realized that he was still deeply affected by the incident and didn't seem to be able to shake it off. "Are you all right?" she asked when he unlocked the door and they entered the trailer. "Please talk to me, Ryder."

"I'll be okay," he said, reaching for her after they both had removed their boots and left them in the hallway. He held her close as if she were a lifeline and it scared her more than his obvious anguish over the incident. "I don't want you to be afraid of me, Summer. I swear with everything that's in me that I'd die before I ever hurt you in any way."

Leaning back, she cupped his lean cheeks with her palms. “It never crossed my mind that you would.”

Sensing that he wouldn’t allow himself to believe her, she tried to think of something that would convince him of her unwavering trust in him. Unable to think of anything she could say to persuade him, she took him by the hand and led him up the steps to the bedroom. Words might not be adequate enough to prove her confidence in him, but actions might.

When they stopped at the side of the bed, Summer turned on the bedside lamp. “Ryder, I need you.”

“Summer, I don’t think this is a good idea…”

“I do,” she said, reaching to unbutton her turquoise blouse. “If you won’t believe me when I tell you how much faith I have in you, then I’m going to show you.”

All things considered, she was a bit surprised by the strength in her own voice. But as she stared up at Ryder, she realized it was true. She not only needed to show him that there wasn’t a single aspect of their relationship that she wasn’t completely sure of or comfortable with, she needed to help him restore his faith in himself.

As she removed the silk garment and reached for the front clasp of her bra, she watched a spark of hunger ignite in the depths of his green eyes. “Darlin’, I don’t want you doing something that you aren’t ready for.”

“I’ve never been more ready for anything in my entire life,” she said, sliding the straps of the silk and lace down her arms.

Rewarded by his rough groan, she looked up to see that the spark in his eyes had ignited into a flame of deep need. Quickly unzipping her jeans before she lost her nerve, she slid them and her panties down her thighs, then stepping out of them, shoved them in the direction of the rest of her clothes.

Summer had thought she might feel some degree of apprehension, but as she stood before Ryder, an emotion unlike anything she had ever experienced before began to fill her. She wasn't just showing him her trust and faith in him, she was laying herself bare both physically and emotionally. She loved Ryder with all her heart and soul and she needed for him to know it.

"You're beautiful," he said, his voice filled with awe.

Reaching for the snaps on his shirt, she made quick work of the closures, then shoved the chambray off his shoulders and tossed it on top of her clothes. "So are you, cowboy," she said, placing her hands on his warm flesh.

He closed his eyes and took a deep breath. When he opened them, he stepped back to take off the rest of his clothes, then reached over to pull her into his arms. The feel of his hard body pressed intimately to hers caused Summer's knees to give way and she had to hold on to his biceps to keep from melting into a puddle at his feet.

"I don't want to scare you, but I need you more right now than I need my next breath," he said, his voice raw with desire.

Without thinking twice, Summer got into bed and held her arms up in invitation. "Make love to me, Ryder."

When he lay down beside her, he immediately wrapped his arms around her and covered her mouth with his. There was a desperation in his kiss, an urgency that she ached to ease.

Moving his lips over hers, then down to the slope of her breast, his mouth closed over her beaded nipple. Writhing with pleasure, she tangled her fingers in the sheets as the sensations he created inside of her threatened to consume her. She felt as if she might burst into flames from the wave of heat sweeping through her when he slid his calloused palm over her abdomen to the most feminine part of her…and she knew she needed him as desperately as he needed her.

"Please make love…to me…Ryder," she gasped as she reached to find him. Stroking him, she wanted him to feel the same excitement, the same hungry anticipation that swirled within her.

She watched him close his eyes and swallow hard as he struggled for control. But when he started to pull her on top of him, she shook her head as she kissed her way down along his strong jaw to his chest, then the thick pads of his pectoral muscles.

"I want to feel you…surround me," she said, lying back against the pillow.

A groan rumbled up from deep in his chest as he nudged her knees apart and settled himself over her. Without hesitation, Summer guided him to her and as she enveloped him with her warmth, her heart felt as if it might burst from the overwhelming emotion filling her. She loved him with every fiber of her being and knew without question that she always would.

When Ryder began to move against her, she welcomed the feeling of his larger body covering hers, making her feel as if she truly had become part of him. But all too soon the urgency of their passion took control and she found herself poised on the edge. Apparently attuned to her needs, he increased the rhythm and depth of the pace he'd set and she suddenly felt herself released from the tension holding her captive. Pleasure, sweet and pure, flowed from the top of her head to the soles of her feet and when Ryder surged into her one final time, it felt as if their souls united.

When he collapsed on top of her, she held him to her and in that moment, she knew without question that she was forever his.

"Are you all right?" he asked as he levered himself to her side.

"I've never been better," she said truthfully. She wanted to tell him she loved him, but she wasn't sure he was ready for that. Instead, she snuggled against him and sighed with contentment. "That was absolutely incredible."

"You're incredible," he said, kissing her until they both gasped for breath.

He held her tightly to him and they were both silent for some time before he finally released her. Clearing his throat, his gaze didn't quite meet hers when he spoke. "I almost forgot to tell you. I got a call from my foreman this afternoon just before the bull riding event. You're going to have to go on to Las Cruces without me. I have to head home tomorrow."

The finality in his voice had her sitting up to tuck the sheet under her arms to cover her breasts. "Is something wrong at the ranch? Is Betty Lou all right? Do you need me to go back with you?"

"No. Betty Lou is fine. It's just ranch stuff. I can handle it." He sat up on the side of the bed and reached for his clothes. "The first thing in the morning, I'll arrange for a charter flight to take you down to Las Cruces."

Her heart seemed to come to a complete halt. "Do you have any idea when you'll be coming back to work?"

Shaking his head, he got to his feet to pull up his jeans. "No."

"Ryder, what's going on?" she asked, tugging the sheet loose to wrap around her as she got out of bed. She had never seen him so stoic or as unwilling to talk to her.

When he turned to face her, she detected a sadness in his eyes that sent a chill up her spine. He quickly shuttered the emotion, replacing it with a look of determination. "Do I really have to spell it out for you, Summer? It was nice while it lasted, but this is over. We're over."

She stared at him in total shock for a moment before she shook her head. "What brought this on? Surely that run-in with Chip Marx—"

"I've changed my mind," he said, cutting her off. "I won't be able to help you with your plan to have a baby after all."

She couldn't believe what was happening. How could everything have fallen apart so fast? And why?

"Don't I even deserve an explanation?" she asked, fighting to keep her emotions under control.

She needed to keep her wits about her in order to

think. Something was going on with him, but for the life of her she couldn't think of what it might be.

"Let's face facts, darlin'. I'm just not cut out to be a daddy and we were only fooling ourselves thinking that I was." He started toward the door. "But now that you've overcome your fears, I'm sure you'll be able to find someone you can settle down with and have a whole houseful of kids."

"Is that…what you really want?" she asked, following him. She hated that she couldn't keep the anguish out of her voice.

"Sure, darlin'." He smiled, but there was a sadness about it that brought tears to her eyes. "Remember? I'm your friend. All I've ever wanted was for you to be happy."

"Where are you going now?" she prodded, desperately trying to think of some way to get him to open up and tell her what was really wrong. She certainly wasn't buying his story that he had changed his mind. He couldn't have made such tender, exquisite love to her and not have it mean anything.

"I'm going out for a while," he said, descending the steps into the main part of the camper. "I don't know what time I'll be back, so don't bother waiting up."

When she watched the door close behind him, Summer felt as if a band tightened around her chest. Why was Ryder shutting her out? Why wouldn't he talk to her?

Tears streamed down her cheeks as she retraced her steps up to the bedroom and sat on the side of the bed. She had never seen him like this. He wasn't the same man she had known and been best friends with for the past few years, the one she trusted above all others. The cowboy she loved.

The man who had just broken her heart was a complete stranger to her.

Nine

Ryder stopped grooming the bay and propped his forearms on the gelding's back to stare at the brush in his hand like it might hold a solution to his problems. After he dropped Summer off at the airport, he had called the rodeo association office and taken an extended leave from his contract commitment with them in order to regain his perspective. But he had been home for a week and his mood still hadn't changed for the better. He was miserable and apparently, without even trying, he was making those around him just as unhappy as he was.

It wasn't that he was irritable and lashed out at anyone. That wasn't his style. Hell, most of the time he tried to keep to himself, either in his office or by taking a ride down to the canyon. But Betty Lou had been hard to avoid. She'd quit at least three times yesterday and once today because she said he was too depressing to be around. Even Lucifer seemed to sense something was wrong and instead of hissing and spitting at him, the cat had rubbed up against Ryder's leg a couple of times as if trying to console him.

But there was nothing anyone could say or do that was going to change the facts. He was here at the Blue Canyon Ranch and Summer was out somewhere on the rodeo circuit. Without him.

Telling her that things were over between them and that he had changed his mind about having a baby with her had been the hardest thing he'd ever had to do in his entire life. But when he lost his temper with Chip Marx and knocked the guy out, it had scared the living hell out of him. All he had been able to think about was the last time he'd thrown a punch in anger. Pete Ledbetter had died because of it and although Ryder had only meant to defend himself and his foster mother, his actions had ended up killing the man. And even if it had been an accident, there was no excuse for it. No one had the right to take another's life.

He wasn't overly proud of the way he handled things that night with Summer either. After punching out Marx, he had realized that he had to let her go, had to let her find happiness with a man who didn't have the kind of baggage he would carry for the rest of his life. But he'd ended up being selfish. He'd had to make love to her one last time before he stepped aside to let her get on with her life, needed to store up one more memory of making love to the woman who would always own him heart and soul.

When his cell phone rang, Ryder groaned. Summer

hadn't tried calling him, but his brothers had. In fact, all five of them had called him at least once a day and sometimes more than that after they learned he had taken a leave of absence from his bullfighting duties on the rodeo circuit.

He knew Nate and Jaron had spread the word about the unfortunate incident and they were all concerned about him. They knew the hell he'd gone through as a teenager as he came to terms with Pete Ledbetter's death and his fear of something like that ever happening again. But as much as they meant to him and as close as they all had been since their days at the Last Chance Ranch, they were the last people he wanted to talk to. He didn't need to hear them tell him that he was making a mountain out of a molehill—or that he was selling Summer short by not telling her about his past and letting her decide for herself what was best.

The bottom line was, he knew he'd done the right thing. They would do well to respect that and leave him alone.

When the phone chirped again he checked the caller ID. His housekeeper probably wanted to tell him she was quitting again.

"What's up, Betty Lou?"

"I think you better come up to the house," she said, sounding a little shaky.

He immediately tossed the brush aside and started toward the barn's double door. "What's wrong?"

"We've got a bit of a situation that you're going to have to handle," she said evasively. "You'd better get up here to the house, pronto."

He'd never heard Betty Lou sound so distressed. "I'm on my way."

The first thing he did as he sprinted across the barnyard was check to see if there was smoke billowing from the house. There wasn't. At least the house wasn't on fire. Then he wondered if Betty Lou had somehow hurt herself. She might have cut herself with a knife while making supper or fallen off the little step stool she used to reach the top shelves in the pantry.

All sorts of disasters ran through his mind and by the time he reached the house, Ryder took the porch steps two at a time. "Betty Lou, are you okay?" he shouted as he jerked open the kitchen door.

Instead of finding Betty Lou bleeding profusely or cradling a broken arm from taking a fall, all five of his brothers sat at the kitchen table, their coffee cups raised in an obviously staged greeting. "Ah, hell," he muttered, glaring at them. He hadn't seen even one of their trucks. If he had, he would have taken off in the opposite direction. "Where did you park?"

"On the other side of the equipment shed," Nate said, grinning.

"We figured you couldn't ignore us if we used the element of surprise," Sam added.

"That was my idea," T.J. chimed in, looking particularly proud of himself.

"And you went along with it, Betty Lou," Ryder accused. "I should fire you for being a traitor."

Unconcerned, Betty Lou shrugged as she turned to stir a big pot on top of the stove. "You can't. I already quit this morning."

"Why don't we get out of Betty Lou's way and go into your office?" Lane suggested, rising from his chair at the table.

"I'd rather not," Ryder said even as he followed his brothers down the hall.

"You know why we're here don't you?" Jaron asked as they filed into the room.

"Yeah, you've dropped by to give me hell over breaking it off with Summer," he said, lowering himself into the chair behind his desk. "But I didn't expect you all to turn it into an intervention."

"It wouldn't have been if you'd taken any of our calls," Sam said as he took a seat on the leather couch.

Fortunately, the office was big enough that the decorator included a couch, as well as the two armchairs in front of his desk. Or maybe in this case, that was unfortunate. There was more than enough room for all of his brothers to sit comfortably while they pointed out the error of his ways.

Glowering at them, he shook his head. "While I appreciate your concern, there's no reason for it. I'll be okay."

"Can it, bro," Jaron spoke up. "If you'll remember, Nate and I were there. We saw how the incident affected you."

"That arrogant bastard didn't give you a choice," Nate added. "He started it and all you did was end it. You were only defending Summer and yourself."

"Yeah and any one of us would have done the same thing," Sam agreed. "If some son of a bitch tried anything like that with Bria, I'd probably have done a whole lot more than just knock out a couple of his teeth."

"A real man doesn't treat a woman like that." T.J. shook his head adamantly. "The jerk needed to be taught a lesson."

"Yeah, but I'd have given anything not to have to be the one teaching the class," Ryder groused.

"How do you feel about what happened?" Lane asked, looking pensive.

Ryder glared at his brother. "Put your psychology degree away, Donaldson. I don't need analysis. I'll be fine."

"Take it from me, you won't be okay until you've talked about it with Summer," Sam advised. "I had to learn my lesson the hard way. Don't be me, Ryder. Don't wait until it's almost too late and you come close to losing her."

Ryder stared at his brother. Sam's stubborn pride had damned near cost him and Bria their marriage and it wasn't until Sam had been injured in an accident that he woke up and realized how much he had to lose. But he and Summer weren't married and it would be easier for him to do the right thing and walk away from her now than it would be later on. He couldn't bear telling her about his past and then watch disillusionment fill her pretty blue eyes when she realized that he wasn't the man she thought him to be.

Before he could set Sam straight and remind him that their situations were different, Lane looked him square in the eye. "Ask yourself what the outcome would have been if you hadn't intervened—both times. Could you have lived with yourself if you'd stood by and let Ledbetter beat his wife to death? Could you have watched Marx while he manhandled Summer and done nothing to stop him?" Checking his watch, he rose to his feet. "I hate to cut this short, but I have an appointment." Turning to the others, he added, "And I believe we've given Ryder a few things he needs to think over."

Watching his brothers file out of the office, Ryder grimaced. One thing about it, his brothers didn't pull any punches. No matter how painful the truth was, they were nothing if not honest with each other.

But they didn't know the whole situation. They weren't aware that Summer had an unshakable belief that he was something he wasn't. She was convinced that he was forthright and incapable of doing any real harm to anyone. The thought of having her find out differently made him feel sick to his stomach.

He would give everything he had to be that man for her. But he couldn't and nothing he could say or do was ever going to change that. He couldn't go back and rewrite his past any more than he could stop the sun from rising in the east each morning.

Unable to sit still, he stalked out of the office and headed back to the barn to saddle the bay. As he rode out of the ranch yard and across the pasture toward the canyon, he knew in his heart that he'd done what was best for her.

His run-in with Marx had turned out all right and had that been the only time he'd had to raise his fists to defend someone, he might feel differently about things.

But he loved Summer too much to saddle her with his youthful mistakes…and a past that he couldn't erase.

Several hours after his brothers left the ranch, Ryder sat beneath the cottonwood tree and watched the breeze cause ripples in the lazy little stream as he tried to figure out what he was going to do with the rest of his life. He couldn't go back to playing chicken with a ton of pissed-off beef. Eventually his and Summer's paths would cross at some rodeo and it would kill him to see her with another man. And there wasn't a doubt in his mind that's exactly what would happen. She was too pretty, too vivacious and full of life not to have a string of men just waiting for the chance to gain her attention.

Leaning back against the tree, he stared up at the gold-colored leaves. His brothers had meant well when they advised him to tell Summer about his past and leave it up to her to decide what was best. But they didn't understand. They had all been in trouble for one thing or another, but robbing a store or running a con game wasn't the same as being responsible for someone's death.

Lost in his own misery, it took a moment for Ryder to realize that someone was approaching on horseback. It was probably one of his men coming to check on the pasture conditions at the far end of the canyon he decided as he got to his feet.

When he looked up, his heart lurched as he watched Summer ride the buckskin mare over beside his bay gelding. Dismounting, she ground tied the horse, then started walking toward him.

"What are you doing here?" he asked, not entirely sure he wasn't dreaming.

From the determined expression on her pretty face, he could tell she was angry. "You owe me an explanation...and I'm not leaving until I get it."

It was all he could do not to take her in his arms and kiss her senseless when she sauntered up to stand in front of him. But that would only further complicate matters. And God only knew everything was complicated enough.

"I don't know what you think I need to explain." It was a barefaced lie. He knew damned good and well what she wanted to know, but it wasn't something she would want to hear.

"Give me a break, cowboy," she said, propping her hands on her shapely hips. "I thought friends were honest with each other."

He took in some much-needed air, then slowly released it. "I'm sorry, darlin', but I don't think I can be your friend anymore."

Her pretty blue eyes narrowed. "Why not?"

"I think you already know the answer to that," he hedged. Why couldn't she just let it go?

"Don't assume that I know anything for certain." Her stubborn little chin was set and he'd seen that expression on her lovely face one too many times not to know that hell would freeze over before she gave up. "I was confident we were best friends and now it appears that's over. I want to know the reason why you ended our friendship. You owe me that much."

Lowering himself to sit at the base of the tree, he shrugged. "We crossed a line and made love."

"I'm well aware of that," she said, sitting on the grass in front of him. "In fact, we crossed that line several times."

"Dammit, Summer, I know how irresistible you are, how responsive," he said, taking off his hat to run his hand over the tension building at the back of his neck. "I can't go back to seeing you every day and not being able to make love to you."

"Who said you had to?" she pressed.

"The deal was that we would make love until you became pregnant," he stated flatly.

"That's true, but that was before," she said, shrugging.

Good Lord she was driving him nuts and she probably didn't even realize it. Or maybe she did and she was determined to make him pay for his transgressions.

"Before what?"

Her expression softened. "Before we fell in love."

She couldn't have shocked him more if she'd tried. "You think we're in love?"

"No, I don't think we are," she said, shaking her head. "I know we are. And I'm here to find out why you're trying to throw away what we have together."

He closed his eyes against the gut-wrenching pain knifing through him. She loved the man she thought he was, not who he really was. In that moment he knew she'd forced his hand and he was going to have to tell her the one thing that would end things between them for good.

"Summer, I'm no good for you," he said, feeling like he had the weight of the world resting on his shoulders. "I'm no good for any woman."

Her honey-blond ponytail swung back and forth as she shook her head. "That's a bunch of garbage. You're the most honest, trustworthy man I've ever known."

"No, I'm not." He took a deep breath. "I haven't been honest with you. I've got a past and it isn't a pretty one, darlin'. You're better off not knowing what I've done."

She met his gaze head-on. "Why don't you tell me about it and let me be the judge of that?"

A knot formed deep in his gut. He was about to see the confidence in her eyes turn to disillusionment and then revulsion. But it was the only way he could convince her that she would be better off without him in her life.

"You know I was a foster kid and finished growing up at the Last Chance Ranch." When she nodded, he swallowed hard. "Do you really want to know why I was sent there?"

"Yes, if that will explain why you think you're not good enough to be in a relationship with me when we both know we're in love."

"I killed a man." Just saying the words caused the knot to twist painfully. "I didn't mean to, but I did."

Her sharp intake of breath made him feel like a piece of his soul had been ripped apart. "My God, Ryder. What happened?"

Telling her about his drunken foster father and the man's habit of beating his wife, Ryder stared down at his balled fists. "When he started to take another swing at my foster mother, I stepped between them. That just pissed him off even more and he drew back to punch me. Because he was drunk he wasn't as steady on his feet and when my fist landed along his jaw, he fell backward." Ryder took a deep breath as the memory of old Pete lying on the floor in a pool of blood ran through his mind. "He hit his head on the kitchen counter, and the next thing I knew he was dead and I was being hauled off to jail and charged with manslaughter."

"That's why you reacted the way you did after that confrontation with Chip Marx, isn't it?" she guessed.

He nodded. "That brought back a lot of bad memories."

"Oh, Ryder, I'm so sorry you had to go through that," she said, surprising him when she rose to her knees to put her arms around him. "But you're being too hard on yourself. Don't you see that the altercation with Marx wasn't your fault any more than it was with your foster father? Both times you were only defending yourself."

"It doesn't bother you that a man died because of me?" he asked, unable to believe she could accept what he'd done.

"Yes, I'm bothered that it happened, but not for the reason you're thinking," she said, cupping his face with her soft palms. "I'm disturbed by the idea that the man tried to hurt you and because of that you've been left feeling that you've done something terribly wrong." She kissed him lovingly. "Yes, it was tragic that the man died, but it was an accident. It's in the past and there's nothing you can do to change that. Don't you think you've punished yourself long enough?"

Wrapping his arms around her, he held her close as he felt a drop of moisture trickle down his cheek. "I can't forget what happened."

Her arms tightened around him. "I'm not saying you should forget. I'm telling you that you didn't do anything wrong and that it's time to stop blaming yourself for the choices other people made. You need to accept and forgive yourself for an unfortunate accident that was out of your control."

Ryder felt free for the first time in years. He wasn't responsible for the actions of others, and although he regretted what happened all those years ago, Summer was right. He needed to look forward instead of living his life regretting the past.

"Did you mean it, Summer?" he asked suddenly.

She looked confused. "What?"

"You said we fell in love." He looked into her crystalline blue eyes. "Do you really love me, darlin'?"

Her smile caused his chest to swell with emotion. "Absolutely. I love you with all my heart and soul, Ryder McClain. You're my best friend and the love of my life. That's something else that you need to accept that's never going to change."

A lump the size of his fist clogged his throat. "Thank God! I love you more than life itself."

Kissing her until he thought they both might pass out from a lack of oxygen, he asked, "Will you marry me, Summer? I want to be the man you go to bed with every night and wake up with every morning. My family will be yours and we'll start our own with a whole houseful of babies." He smiled. "I give you my word, you'll never be alone again. I'll be with you until the day I die."

To his relief, there wasn't a moment's hesitation in her answer. "Yes." Her smile was the sweetest he had ever seen. "But there's something I need to tell you, cowboy."

Holding her to his chest, he kissed the top of her head then the tip of her nose. "What's that, darlin'?"

"I'm thrilled I'll finally be part of a big family," she said, giving him a watery smile. "And just so you know, you were right about those swimmers."

Ryder frowned. "What are you talking about?"

"We've already started on that houseful of babies," she said, grinning.

He felt his heart come to a complete halt, then start thumping hard against his ribs. "You're pregnant?"

"I haven't seen a doctor yet, but the test I bought at the pharmacy says I am," she said, nodding.

He couldn't stop grinning. "It looks like Bria's sister, Mariah, and Jaron will have two reasons to argue about babies and whether they'll be boys or girls."

When she touched his cheek, he felt like the luckiest man in the entire world. "I love you, cowboy."

"And I love you, darlin'." He rose to his feet, then held out his hand to help her up. When she placed her hand in his, he felt as if he'd been handed a rare and precious gift. "Let's go back to the house. We have a few phone calls to make."

"Your brothers?" she asked.

He laughed. "I can't remember the last time I knew something about myself that they didn't know first."

Epilogue

"I'm telling you, they'll both be girls, Jaron Lambert," Mariah insisted.

Jaron stubbornly shook his head. "And I'm telling *you,* they're going to be boys."

Ryder stood with his brothers, watching Mariah and Jaron debate the gender of the babies Summer and Bria were going to have. "Do you think it's crossed their minds that we might have one of each?"

Sam shrugged as he took a swig of beer from the bottle in his hand. "I doubt it. I don't think it matters to either one of them what sex the babies are. They just like to argue."

"So who's next?" T.J. asked, grinning like a fool.

"Next for what?" Nate asked, distracted. He had his eye on a willowy redhead across the dance floor, and

Ryder was glad to see that his brother had finally gotten over that little nurse up in Waco and was moving on.

"The next to get married, genius," T.J. shot back.

"My money is on you and that neighbor of yours, T.J.," Lane said with a grin.

"I keep telling you, I'd rather go buck naked for eight seconds on a porcupine than to take up with the likes of her," T.J. said, shaking his head. "She's still letting that stud of hers jump the fence and get with my mares."

Ryder blocked out his brother's complaints about his neighbor and the horse she couldn't seem to keep at home as he scanned the crowd, looking for his wife. When he spotted her in that gorgeous white wedding gown, he caught his breath. He doubted there would ever be a time that the sight of her didn't have that effect on him.

"It might be you, Lane," Ryder said, checking his watch. Another hour and it should be socially acceptable for him to take his bride and leave the wedding reception to start their honeymoon.

"Getting married isn't part of my life plan," Lane quipped. "The ranch I won last month in that poker game in Shreveport is as close to settling down as I intend to get."

They all looked at Nate for a moment. His attention had already turned from the redhead to a curvy brunette.

"That's a sucker bet if I ever saw one," Lane said, laughing.

"While you all carry on about who the next will be to take dip in the marital pool with me and Sam, I'm going to dance with my wife," Ryder announced, turning to walk across the dance floor.

When he approached Summer, her smile caused his body to tighten and he wished like hell they were already on that island in the Caribbean where they were spending their honeymoon. "Could I have this dance, darlin'?"

She placed her hand in the crook of his arm as she smiled up at him. "This one and all of the dances for the rest of my life."

"That's sounds like a good idea to me," he murmured, taking her in his arms. When she rested her head against his chest, he kissed her forehead. "Are you happy, Summer?"

"I've never been happier, Ryder." Leaning back to look up at him, the love shining in the depths of her eyes sent his hormones into overdrive. "You've given me every one of my dreams."

"And you'vc given me every one of mine, darlin'." He grinned. "All except for one."

"Which one is that?" she asked, clearly intrigued.

"As beautiful as you look in your wedding gown, when you were walking down the aisle toward me, all I could do was stand there and daydream about the moment I get to take it off you," he whispered close to her ear.

She shivered against him and he knew she was looking forward to starting their lives together as much as he was. "I've been dreaming about you doing that, too." Smiling, she kissed him tenderly. "I love you, cowboy."

"And I love you, darlin'." Grinning, he took her by

the hand and started toward the door. "Now, let's go somewhere a little more private and I'll see what I can do about making both of our dreams come true."

* * * * *

COMING NEXT MONTH from Harlequin Desire®

AVAILABLE AUGUST 6, 2013

#2245 CANYON

The Westmorelands

Brenda Jackson

When Canyon Westmoreland's ex-lover returns to town, child in tow and needing a safe haven, he's ready to protect what's his, including the son he didn't know he had.

#2246 DEEP IN A TEXAN'S HEART

Texas Cattleman's Club: The Missing Mogul

Sara Orwig

When tradition-bound Texas millionaire Sam Gordon discovers the sexy set designer he shared a passionate night with is pregnant, he proposes. But Lila Hacket won't settle for anything but the real deal—it's true love or bust!

#2247 THE BABY DEAL

Billionaires and Babies

Kat Cantrell

A baby can't be harder than rocket science! But when aerospace billionaire Michael Shaylen inherits a child, he realizes he needs expert help—from the woman who once broke his heart.

#2248 WRONG MAN, RIGHT KISS

Red Garnier

Molly Devaney has been forbidden to Julian Gage his entire life. But when she asks him to help her seduce his brother, Julian must convince her *he's* the man she really wants.

#2249 HIS INSTANT HEIR

Baby Business

Katherine Garbera

When the man who fathered her secret baby comes back to town with plans to take over her family's business, Cari Chandler is suitably shell-shocked. What's a girl to do—especially if the man is irresistible?

#2250 HIS BY DESIGN

Dani Wade

Wedding white meets wedding night when a repressed executive assistant at a design firm finds herself drawn to the unconventional ideas and desires of her new boss.

HDCNM0713

Canyon Westmoreland is about to get the surprise of his life!
Don't miss a moment of the drama in
CANYON
by New York Times *and* USA TODAY *bestselling author*
Brenda Jackson
Available August 2013
only from Harlequin® Desire®!

Canyon watched Keisha turn into Mary's Little Lamb Day Care. He frowned. Why would she be stopping at a day care? Maybe she had volunteered to babysit for someone tonight.

He slid into a parking spot and watched as she got out of her car and went inside, smiling. Hopefully, her good mood would continue when she saw that he'd followed her. His focus stayed on her, concentrating on the sway of her hips with every step she took, until she was no longer in sight. A few minutes later she walked out of the building, smiling and chatting with the little boy whose hand she was holding—a boy who was probably around two years old.

Canyon studied the little boy's features. The kid could be a double for Denver, Canyon's three-year-old nephew. An uneasy feeling stirred his insides. Then, as he studied the little boy, Canyon took in a gasping breath. There was only one reason the little boy looked so much like a Westmoreland.

Canyon gripped the steering wheel, certain steam was coming out of his ears.

He didn't remember easing his seat back, unbuckling his

HDEXP73258

seat belt or opening the car door. Neither did he remember walking toward Keisha. However, he would always remember the look on her face when she saw him. What he saw on her features was surprise, guilt and remorse.

As he got closer, defensiveness followed by fierce protectiveness replaced those other emotions. She pulled her son—the child he was certain was *their* son—closer to her side. "What are you doing here, Canyon?"

He came to a stop in front of her. His body was radiating anger from the inside out. His gaze left her face to look down at the little boy, who was clutching the hem of Keisha's skirt and staring up at him with distrustful eyes.

Canyon shifted his gaze back up to meet Keisha's eyes. In a voice shaking with fury, he asked, "Would you like to tell me why I didn't know I had a son?"

HDEXP73258